PRAISE FOR *LET G*
THE DEAD

"Darrin Doyle's brilliant *Let Gravity Seize the Dead* is both wizardry and wildfire. Doyle's rich and evocative words conjure other worlds, beyond this one, beyond life and death. I read this book both breathlessly and with rapid breathing—taking in too little and too much air—as the narrative moved between time periods and as family secrets unraveled, whistled, and called out from one generation to the next. Like the best of Poe, like Henry James' *The Turn of the Screw*, like Denis Johnson's *Train Dreams*, this book lures us in, alters our perception, and leaves us haunted."

—Kelcey Ervick, author of *The Keeper*

"Darrin Doyle's *Let Gravity Seize the Dead* is about a family who builds a house deep in the Michigan woods and then keeps returning to it, in body, in mind, for reasons they can't bring themselves to understand until it might be too late. It's one of the spookiest, most headlong books I've ever read. It might remind you, as it did me, of Shirley Jackson's *We Have Always Lived at the Castle* and also of Stephen King's *The Shining*. But really, it's all

Darrin Doyle, who for years has been writing marvelous books about our best intentions and our worst impulses. This is his best yet. Fair warning, though: once you start reading, you won't be able to stop."

—Brock Clarke, author of *Who Are You, Calvin Bledsoe?*

"With *Let Gravity Seize the Dead*, Darrin Doyle has fashioned a story of compelling Faulknerian intensity, the evil in it emerging not just from the sins of the past but a Michigan landscape with as much malevolent presence as Annie Proulx's *Wyoming*. It's an insidious and infecting evil, an atonal whistle at night reminding you that the forests still hide the darkness our ancestors feared."

—Naeem Murr, author of *The Perfect Man*

"'Want to know a person, look under the soil. That's where the story is,' Darrin Doyle writes in his grim and tautly interwoven ghost story, *Let Gravity Seize the Dead*. Violence and trauma may run deep as the forest roots through the Randall family property, but so does Doyle's gift of language, which haunts these lean pages with lines like 'window tarps flap like flightless birds in the night wind,' to deliver a moody, pitch dark novella that will linger in my nightmares for quite some time."

—Sara Lippman, author of *Lech*

"In gorgeous, mesmerizing language, Darrin Doyle's *Let Gravity Seize the Dead* vividly traces generations of a family haunted by the horrors of place and confronting, as will readers, stark, brute truths about a beautiful but unforgiving reality."

—Matt Roberson, author of *Impotent*

"Electric, engrossing, and immaculately written, Darrin Doyle's seventh book is a triumphant addition to the American novella canon. Set in a lush landscape where 'horseflies buzz like airplanes' and 'dead trees wear mushrooms like necklaces,' this mystery/ghost story/Gothic dollop of haunted domesticity will grab you by the throat and refuse to let go until the last page is turned."

—David James Poissant, author of *Lake Life* and *The Heaven of Animals*

LET GRAVITY SEIZE THE DEAD

Darrin Doyle

Regal House Publishing

Published by
Regal House Publishing, LLC
Raleigh, NC 27605
All rights reserved

ISBN -13 (paperback): 9781646034451
ISBN -13 (epub): 9781646034468
Library of Congress Control Number: 2023943418

Cover images and design by © C. B. Royal
Regal House Publishing, LLC
https://regalhousepublishing.com

Printed in the United States of America

For Courtney

First time the sisters heard it they thought bird. Pitch night though is when the whistler blew, and not much birdsong lived under moonlight. Even city girls could tell you that. Next, they considered coyote, a female in distress or a pup. But no canine carries notes so tuneful and sad. Sad maybe but not tuneful.

The cabin set back from County Road 93 more than two miles, the only access a lurching dirt one-lane, unpredictably divoted and cloaked by evergreens. Visitors when they came—which was not often and then primarily postal carriers—took up to twenty minutes to lose their sea legs from that road. No other cabins or homes existed along the stretch, which is why the Randalls thought of it as their own private path to the world.

Trees stood close-woven, even when hardwoods lost their leaves. Lean pines, black and jack, formed dark mazes, needle beds soft in their perpetual shade. Armies of that pine flanked the plot that Beck Randall's great-grandparents had cleared in 1900. No power tools back then. Just Loren and Betty daybreak until night, chopping, sawing, and hauling, laying hammer and planer to wood, mosquitoes an unbroken whine, plagues of gnat and black fly. Ticks like little chocolate drops each evening plucked with tweezers. Haze of sawdust fog-binding the world. Neighbors of no one, the nearest town Wolfolk four miles distant. Stories had it that raising cabin, shed, and pole barn took near a decade and shortened Loren Randall's life to forty-six years.

Loren died in his bed after a long fever. Pneumonia is what the country doctor named it. Bernie and Lucille by that time were teenager and almost-teenager, respectively. They hovered bedside with their mother as Loren's life passed out of his body and he released his final words: "Now I'm a branch."

The phrase lived in Lucille's mind for her remaining life, along with the image of her father ghosted on the sheets. Once a brick-strong man, he'd turned mulch. His wet eyes had located Lucille's. As a child, she didn't understand her father's look or his final words, though in time she came to understand his shame and pity, what past he had lived and future he foresaw.

During construction the children were too little to help but old enough to keep out of the way. Daylight hours they retreated into the woods with satchels of butter sandwiches and apples, wandering until the saws and chops of trees called no louder than the bugs. Bernie with his slingshot, Lucille brandishing a walking stick twice her height for imaginary highwire-crossing.

She had seen a sketch of a highwire walker in a book, his long horizontal pole bent like a frown. The wire-walker was stepping with a relaxed face as if a chasm didn't yawn beneath him like a giant's throat. She believed the wire-walker real no matter what her brother said.

Bernie, meanwhile, launched rocks at moving targets, mostly chipmunks too quick or birds that on rare occasion perished in feathery explosions.

Bernie told stories about the forest eater. "The trees are his teeth," he said. "He'll chew you up. No one will see you again."

Lucille thought the story funny. Funny to see the woods as the great wide-open mouth. She would scream, *I'm on its tongue* while wire-walking a fallen elm.

But when dusk crept in and shadow quilted the forest floor, she sprinted back to Ma and Pa and threw her arms around them and asked for cocoa even in the heart of summer.

Betty lived to ninety-one, her final thirty-six years alone in that cabin after Loren died and then Bernie died, and then Lucille fled downstate. When Betty passed, her body wasn't found for eleven days. The mail truck stopped by only monthly. Her heart had expired near the pole barn while cleaving wood for the stove, even at her advanced age performing most chores herself. Because what choice did she have, she against the forest? Because here was her home. Because here she had planted life. Coyotes fed on Betty until she was bone.

Lucille receiving this news understood that poor Bernie (whose dead face haunted her) had been correct: the woods had eaten their ma after all.

The cabin stood empty for decades, waist-deep in scrub and weeds by the time Beck Randall purchased it from his own father, son of Lucille. Beck's father had been willed the eighty acres but never so much as stepped onto the property. Viewed it only in grainy photographs.

Beck's father was an elderly, semi-retired Detroit tax attorney with no interest in outdoor life. His mother, Jewish Brooklyn-born-and-raised, influenced his father's interests and disposition in ways both profound and trivial, casting a shadow of disrespect upon Beck's image of his father.

An only child, Beck happily spent his and his wife's savings, including a portion of the college fund, to buy both cabin and land. His father charged market value.

Acreage surrounding the Randall property sold on occasion, but nobody constructed upon it. Purchasers discovered the environs unkind, too serried to clear, beyond reach of creature comfort. Plots were used for hunting or not at all.

Beck moved there with Mallory and their teenage daughters. The four hacked brush, working blisters into their hands just like Loren and Betty, sweating the soil, Beck and Mallory feeling good about connecting— with their girls, with the earth—about breathing air unchanged in the past century plus. Hired a contractor to do what they couldn't. Six months of labor: new roof laid, a section of wall rebuilt, faux-wood flooring installed, modern appliances, sinks and fixtures, electrical rewiring, a furnace.

The interior was cozy: two bedrooms, kitchen, living area, bathroom.

The exterior, greenish hue of the pines and peeling like sunburned skin, got scraped and redone in apple red at the request of Tina. At thirteen, she had an artist's eye.

"The last page of my obituary will be a poem," Tina said. "I'm working on it right now."

"Don't be stupid. Nobody writes their own obituary." Lucy was not in the mood. Whimsy, whimsy. Tina's teacher, who was now their mother, rewarded Tina for whimsy, had in effect labeled it her youngest daughter's life calling.

Meanwhile, Lucy's calling according to Mother was to be a human calculator. The girl despised math and wished she didn't find it so easy.

Weekdays, the Randall daughters did schoolwork at the kitchen table unless the sun was shining like now. A rarity, a pleasant distraction, the dazzling milky glow. On the wooden swing they swayed, read, and typed on laptops that were tough to read in the glare.

"Tina Elizabeth Randall," Tina recited from her computer, "passed away combatively on Thursday evening. She was seventeen years old and had no desire to expire. She attempted to stave off the Grim Reaper through invented rhymes and profanities—a filibuster, if you will. Sadly, her strategy worked only for a few hours and ultimately her dry throat did her in. Tina's life, although tragically brief, will be remembered by all who came into contact with her. Her spirit was wise beyond her ears, her eyes, all her organs. Some said she was the reincarnation of every daffodil that ever flowered in the northern hemisphere. Others claimed she had hatched from a robin's egg. On the hour her body gave itself to the earth, the trees sang, the birds bloomed, the sky was brown and the soil blue. Insects shed their fur and grew to the size of clouds while forest mammals assembled a chain of bones from their dead and circled the world three times over."

"That's not a poem," Lucy said. "And how do you know the word filibuster?"

The screen door thwacked, meaning Mother had sandwiches. She squinted in the sun while setting plates on the side table by the swing. "Your father is going to be sad that he missed this day."

Beck was at work. He had moved his family out here, away from everything and everyone, and ended up as a fry cook in Wolfolk. An electrical engineer by trade, he liked to say that nobody lived around here and they all were hiring. Tina laughed at the joke while Lucy read her fingernails.

"Maybe we should film this day for him," Tina said. "I'll start recording now." She stared out at the weed-free lot, the sparkling wheelbarrow, the buttering flit terflies (as she called them). Her flat expression, Lucy supposed, was meant to emulate a camera's emotion-less objectivity.

Mother humored Tina, as usual: "Your dad will love it."

The ghost of Bernie walked these woods. And great-great grandma Betty roamed the yard. This is what Tina liked to say since they arrived.

What about Loren? was Lucy's question. And what about Lucille?

Tina shrugged. "I haven't heard from them."

❧

In some areas of the forest, carcasses of fallen trees leaned on each other for support. Pads of moss spotted the earth. Soft to the touch, fuzzy. Mossy trunks, mossy hollow logs. Bernie explained that moss was a living creature like you and me, and he pointed at Lucille, and Lucille laughed because she was thinking about what it would be like to be a fungus that existed only to overtake and never love or bleed.

A sun-hot afternoon. Patches of briar bush the children waded through snagged at their trousers, trying to grab and keep them. The children reached an overlook. A pond waited at the foot of a steep slope. Bernie helped his sister descend; carefully they stepped, leaning into the hill, not wanting to tumble.

They reached the bottom. Squatted at the pond. Dipped fingers to feel the chill. Scoured shoreline in search of rocks with eyes or slimy backs peeking from the gloom. Bernie could catch them; Lucille was too slow. His hand hovered, steady. Waiting. Bernie was none too bright but had patience. The wind carried faraway trills. A squirrel scampered into brush. Then down slammed Bernie's hand, cupping the frog before it could escape. Tenderly he squeezed. He let Lucille touch its pulsing throat. She tried to read its eyes but found only black orbs, blank and unmindful. Perhaps this was nature's ploy, its survival strategy, to live without feeling. If you had no feelings, you couldn't be destroyed. Even young Lucille understood this. She'd seen her father's eyes.

"God gave dominion to man," Bernie said. "I have to show these creatures the way it is. It's my Christian duty."

"You're not a Christian," Lucille said. "Or a man."

"I ought to eat this critter." He faced the frog to his lips, opened his mouth to let the animal see its future.

"He doesn't have ears. Just little holes."

"*You* don't have ears."

"What?" she said.

"You don't have ears."

"What?"

"I said, YOU DON'T HAVE EARS."

Lucille lost it, laughing. Bernie was so stupid. Off she ran, scampering on all fours up the slope, imagining herself an animal, gripping trees for leverage, sweating as she crested the top. Below, Bernie was the size of a marble. The pond weeds were stubby hairs like on Pa's face. Sunshine flared on the glassy surface. Breeze wrinkled the water, reflected grass like wriggling tails. Everything alive out here. Everything forever.

&

Beck and Mallory knew their girls were missing out. On life, on social events, on camaraderie with peers.

Lucy was a sixteen-year-old dragged away from friends, relocated like a captive animal and released into the wild. She had argued and cried and found no support from Tina or her parents. It's a democracy, her dad kept saying, and you're outvoted.

"We're starting over," her mother said with a spark in her eye, her endless optimism like a robotic glitch in her brain.

I never started the first time, was Lucy's thought. She kept the thought inside, however, decided to keep all her thoughts from now on—her only private space in this cramped cottage.

Evenings after the girls went to bed, Beck and Mallory played cards at the dinner table. The odor of fried cod clung to Beck, his nightly cologne. The television's quiet cacophony punctuated the drone of crickets outside.

"To four months," Mallory said, raising her wine.

A clink and a drink. "How are your students?" Beck said. The merlot was beginning to turn so he drank it in a gulp, made a face, felt his blood heat.

"Lucy isn't happy."

"Happiness is the great American myth."

"She's lonely, Beck."

Beck played his card, a spade. "I win."

In the girls' room, night sang with September heat. Late night, the cricketsong stopped and the quiet became a throttling of sound. Threads of a spider web or blanket brushed Lucy's cheek. She heard the tick of the wall clock. Sheets sweaty.

"You aren't asleep," Tina whispered from the darkness, "and I can't wake up." She giggled.

Lucy didn't answer, was tired of answering. Every night, Tina talked.

Lucy heard the rustle of covers and was greeted bedside by a moonlit face.

"Let's go find the whistler."

"You're dreaming. Go back to bed."

"Dad says we're all dreaming here. Every day is a dream, and every night we die."

"Then shut up and let me die."

"I made up that last part because I'm scared to die."

"You won't die until you're seventeen. I heard your obituary."

"I think Bernie died when he was little. Like almost a baby."

"You know that's not true."

"I can learn things from the way my head itches."

"This is so fun."

"Is the forest in my skin?"

"Smells like it."

"Do you think we'll hear the whistler tonight?"

"Not if we're dead. Go to sleep."

Not enough English language to describe the shades of green. Lily pad, thunderstorm cloud. Jack pine like a bristled dragon tongue. Green as a bruise, as cough syrup, as spinach boiled and raw. As opossum guts exposed to sun. Swamp water, baby waste, duck waste, northern lights braiding a midnight sky.

"Why would anybody choose to live out there?" Beck's father had asked.

"I'm not anybody," was Beck's answer.

They sat in the living room, Beck with his father and mother.

"You won't find work," his mother said. Her tone suggested fact not speculation.

"There are other things to find," Beck said.

His father cracked open a pistachio, dropped the pale green nut into his mouth. Squat little man in a diamond-patterned sweater. Age had shrunk his body but not his intensity. Smacked his lips when he chewed, even a tiny nut. Beck wanted nothing from his father except this, and he wanted this to be nothing. His father, though, could never issue a blessing without critique.

The fireplace churned with flame, gas fire born from the turn of a switch. Everything in Beck's childhood home was automatic, flipped off and on.

"Our son the hippie," his dad said.

"We won't see our granddaughters anymore." Another fact from Mother's frowning face, testing Beck's guilt. She was a fusty woman with bony hands, lean as a flagpole, a fanatical homemaker twenty years her father's junior. All Beck's life they had enjoyed talking near one another.

"You'll see the girls when you choose to," Beck assured her. His response was measured, determined not to get riled.

"He's talking about pictures and phone calls," his father said, acting like Beck wasn't in the room. "He can't expect us to drive out there." His father's eyes flickered in the light. His set lips bespoke an internal struggle. "Do you even know what happened at that place? I'm not selling it to you. Final answer."

Beck squeezed the arms of the recliner. He felt like he was falling. He looked meaningfully at his father, then his mother. Then back again. He wanted his father to sense what he was thinking.

"You sure?" Beck said. He held the trump card.

Cards, plural. "You seem concerned about the past. About old forgotten shit."

Beck would not turn away when his father's expression hardened. Mother was checking her phone.

Bernie and Lucille play a game. A nighttime game. Bernie says it's called *Find the Whistle*.

Pa is snoring. The children hear saws all day every day. At night their pa becomes a saw in his dreams. The cabin is a skeleton without muscle or flesh. The family sleeps in wooden bones under wool blankets, breathing the detritus of timber. Window tarps flap like flightless birds in the night wind. On the table, Pa's whiskey bottle overshadows an empty glass.

Flannel shirts pulled over flannel pajamas. Careful of the hinge that squeaks. The children step outside.

Shock smell of humid sawdust and pine. Moths swarm Bernie's light. Bernie grips Lucille's hand, not letting go. She wants to hold on but wants to be free. Wants both. She's not scared and has never been except when her pa grabbed Bernie by the throat. So long ago and far away that it feels like a dream.

No wind. No stars. Just those perfect forest soldiers at the ready, black rows deeper than sight, haunting beyond the lantern glow.

They tramp along no path. Even barefoot children snap branches, crunch needles. They are the loudest life. Lucille senses, all around, birds and chipmunks and squirrels and raccoons and opossum: in trees, in brush, cowering at the storm of their tread. Her blood rushes.

"Where are we going?"

"Right here." Bernie frees her damp hand.

Here is nowhere. Ground thick with knee-high ferns. Spring peepers chirping in the marsh, gray tree frog throating like a rattle. No breeze, waned moon. Bloom of yellowsoft lamp shine, mist on the air.

"Close your eyes," Bernie says.

"Why?"

"You're in bed sleeping. Close your eyes."

Bernie wouldn't hurt her. Lucille knows. There's light inside her brother, a dull spark like a black rock struck by sun. The lantern flame bends against the dark.

She obeys. On her eyelids shadows dance. She hears Bernie padding through brush.

"Walk sideways," he whispers, now maybe fifteen feet off. Does fear quiver his words? "You have to go in sideways or the mouth thinks you're food and swallows you. Here. Stop. Have you opened your eyes?"

"No."

"A little?"

"No."

"Crouch now. Hands and knees. You can't see me, but I'm crawling too."

"I don't like this."

"It's okay. Scared is part of it."

She crawls blind. The ground is scrolling. She's crawling but isn't moving. Someone is behind her, at her heels. She can't escape. She's swimming a black world without eyes. Hands throttle her calves and she gasps.

It's Bernie. He says to stand up and keep her eyes closed.

"Come out," he whispers. He isn't talking to Lucille. "It's okay. Come out. I want you to meet my sister."

Homeschooling was a cakewalk compared to real schooling. A classroom with a sky ceiling. Less work, self-directed. No cafeteria food or bathroom passes. But Lucy could never admit these joys to her mom. Only when Mother came upon her unannounced did Lucy show a face without dour lips.

Lucy knew the future. Friends would forget her. Would stop calling and texting. Not right away, maybe not for a while. But it would happen. Gradually they would have nothing to talk about. No shared experi-ences. In-jokes, memories: autumn leaves shriveling without sound. Her old life would end not in pain but something worse. A quiet attrition, a decomposition until she was replaced by a new self.

She missed boys. No boys in particular, but the idea of them. Energy wafting from their skin. Stupid clueless faces that made them surprisingly attractive. Musky smell after PE. Childish sexual puns that Lucy smiled at in spite of herself. Inappropriate laughs behind the teachers' backs. Lucy was no troublemaker but loved watching others make trouble. Thrilling when a boy would misbehave and under threat of detention double down—telling the teacher to *suck it* or whatever words found their mouths. They were spontaneous emotion, rage, and humiliation weaponized.

Sure, girls did the same thing. But Lucy understood how their minds worked, which took away the shine.

And anyway, there were no girls out here either. Except Tina. Brilliant, babyish Tina. Tina who almost broke the floor bouncing up and down when she heard they were vanishing into a Michigan wilderness to live with beavers and poison ivy.

Lucy's cellphone got a couple bars. Not all the time. Her dad didn't even own a phone. Got rid of it when they moved. Tina had never owned one. Only Lucy and her mom. Mom loved emailing pictures to show off their perfect family—which, what did Lucy know?

Maybe this *was* the perfect family. Maybe this was the best possible life. Maybe life, in its ideal form, basically sucked.

Mom told relatives they MUST visit because they would simply LOVE IT. Never mind that her relations lived seven states away and never left their towns and the cabin had no room for guests anyway, so what the goddamn hell?

Beck's father reached across the desk after the transaction. Stiffly shook hands as if he'd pawned off a car on a stranger. His father's palm was hard and dry. Underactive sweat glands.

"This right here is what I call an idiotic move," his father said, congratulating Beck on his idiocy. The man was elderly but his blazing eyes shook you.

Beck tucked the deed into the bulging accordion folder with maps, insurance information, architectural schematics, manuals for furnace and appliances.

Beck's father tucked the cashier's check into his own thinner folder. A meticulous record-keeper, his father. Meticulous money-earner. Meticulous everything, even at the cusp of ninety. His brain made tacks seem dull.

"You know what happened out there, right?" His father poured a short glass of seltzer from the bottle on his desk. He drank buckets of the stuff, claiming it would give him erections to a hundred. Digestion, his father said, was key. His father, obsessed with longevity, was nearly fifty when Beck was born. His sworn enemy was time. He called aging *decaying* and ran five miles every morning with the speed and gait of a man fleeing a crime scene. Beck didn't ask about the erections.

"You've told me, yes."

"It doesn't bother you?"

"It was a century ago."

Beck's father sniffed, a wordless rebuke. The office walls were decorated with framed pictures of his father on his boat, hoisting big lake fish. Proud like he'd conquered the world. Beck had never caught a fish. There were no pictures of Beck or his mother.

"Please visit once in a while," his father said, staring into fizzy water. His tone was uncharacteristic, vulnerable. Not pleading but close. "Your mother doesn't want to lose her granddaughters."

Beck nodded, pleased, knowing they were already lost.

❧

"Where did you find him? He's lovely."

"Don't remember."

"You caught him?"

"Dad showed me how to make a trap because I'm a boy."

A black rabbit huddled in the corner of the crude cage of spare boards. When Bernie lifted the top of the box the animal remained motionless but for a twitch of its nose. Its dull ebony coat camouflaged the ears flat against its head.

"Ma would love that fur for a hat."

Bernie leaned over the box, dirty hands on knees. "I was gonna cut his throat but he smiled at me."

In the distance the wind roared, a river through the treetops. The forest talked, their father liked to say. Shouldn't usually listen.

"Will she smile at me?" Lucille reached into the box the way she was taught to greet dogs, without threat. The animal's nose vibrated. Its eyes were somehow blacker than its coat. In the box, pellets mixed with grass clumps.

"It's a *he*," Bernie said. "I wouldn't keep no girl."

"Will he smile at me?"

"He has human teeth."

"Nu-uh."

"Dare you to look."

Lucille stroked the fur. Shockingly soft, like her ma's hair. She realized how much she loved her ma and pa and missed them even though she saw them working outside every day.

Bernie said, "He whistles too."

"Rabbits don't whistle."

"Like a person. He was stuck in my snare. Probably figured he was gonna die. Started whistling real sad."

The rabbit looked at Lucille. She felt a tremor, an opening of space, the hardness inside her eroding. This animal was menacing or inviting, she couldn't tell. Each possibility spiked her lungs.

She stood. "He can't be caught."

Bernie slapped the lid back in place. "Shouldn't have let himself."

Alaina's was a FAMILY RESTAURANT in all-caps, which Beck knew was no indication of quality. Still, he expected a semblance of the food his mother had never made but his friends' mothers had. Home cooking that is. Instead, what Alaina's served arrived in semis and needed only to be unpackaged and warmed in microwaves or dipped in hot oil for x minutes. Even the spaghetti sauce came in industrial-sized cans. Working at Alaina's made Beck appreciate Mallory that much more.

In fact as he sucked at his break-time Camel it aston-

ished him the lengths Mallory had gone to—sacrifices
she had made—to take this ride. He didn't understand,
didn't feel called to understand, the reasons behind his
compulsion to spend their savings on the remote cabin
and acreage. Didn't understand why he was willing to
quit a stable career designing, installing, and updating
lighting systems in retirement homes, community cen-
ters, hospitals. Didn't understand why his resolve in-
vigorated when Lucy begged him to let her finish high
school before they moved.

Beck didn't know his own motives and equally didn't
apprehend his wife's when she followed with no resistance, only encouragement.

Of course he had asked: Why are you agreeing to
this?

And of course Mallory said love. Love, adventure, a
wish to not live without living.

But for Beck her answer only proved that he didn't
know his wife at all. Her unselfish acquiescence both
attracted and disgusted. If she had asked him to quit
his career and move to the center of nowhere; if she
had asked him to homeschool their girls and become
a househusband—he would have laughed. Laughed
at her stupidity. Laughed like his father. And if she
had continued to press him who knows what else. He
wasn't sure if stubbornness made him a great man or

the opposite. His well was too dark and airless to reach by lantern—as was true, Beck reasoned, with every person. So why try?

A waitress stepped out the door and kicked the wood block back into place so they wouldn't be locked out. Her angular body appeared too long for her uniform. After a theatrical rainbow of arms stretching above her head, she located a cigarette in her apron and lit it.

"Even when it's not busy it's busy," she said.

Beck studied the dumpster, wondered who had settled on the color shit-brown and why.

"Your daughter go out for sports?" she said.

"Which one?"

Her graying hair was trying to escape its bun, a few strands succeeding. She squinted against the smoke as she removed her flat-soled shoe and whacked a pebble free. "How many you got?"

"Two. Feels like twenty." He didn't really mean it, but he had dealt with blue-collar workers and knew how to make platitudes that would pass as conversation. Complaining about family was a go-to.

The waitress chuckled as Beck knew she would. "Got three myself. Two girls and a boy. We never actually met. Different shifts. I'm Shelley."

He shook her hand and said, "Beck. I know your name because it's on your tag."

She seemed to be assessing his age. "Your girls at the high school?"

"Homeschooled," he said. He stepped on his cigarette. "Sixteen and thirteen."

"That right? I could never teach nobody." In the dusk light her thin frame and bone structure made her cadaverous.

"The wife is the professor." Beck opened the door to return to mozzarella sticks and onion rings. "I got my own career to worry about." He winked and was followed inside by Shelley's smoky cackle.

Horseflies here buzz like airplanes.

Dead trees wear mushrooms like necklaces.

Simile: a comparison between two fundamentally different things.

Prickers grab socks or socks grab prickers.

Death in life or life in death.

Palindrome: a word or phrase that reads the same backward as forward.

Lucy and Tina had found the photo album under their parents' bed. This was a few years before they moved to the cabin. The girls had seen pictures of themselves, naturally: baby Tina and toddler Lucy. Photos of picnics, birthdays, beaches. Lives arranged like a comic book.

But this album they had never seen. It was a thin book the shade of gravy. Tina had been trying on her mom's jewelry and dropped an earring beside the bed.

"What made you pull out this book?" Lucy, turning pages, wanted to know.

Tina frowned. "It was the only thing under the bed."

"Bullshit."

"Bull true!"

"Just this?" She waved the book. "That's not possible."

The Randall parents were not organized. Clutter grew like fungus throughout the house.

At the kitchen table, Lucy and Tina flipped through the album. Black and whites exclusively. Ancient turn-of-the century portraits of the stern and sullen. People like stone or soap carvings. No smile to be seen. Pale, in overalls or dark formal dresses. Children tight-eyed, caught like deer in the flash. All of them dead now.

Lucy peeled the plastic to free a few photos from the black corner mounts. Names and dates were scrawled on the backs:

Loren and Betty Randall 1903
Betty Randall 1905
Bernie and Lucille Randall 1907
Wolfolk cabin 1907

"She looks like Dad," Tina said. She touched Lucille, a girl of about ten years.

"They're related, duh."

"Are you named after her?"

"I don't know." Lucy had never heard of this relative. None of these people. How was this possible? Who were they? Lucy had always hated her first name, and to learn she'd been named after a relative she never knew existed? Angry confusion found purchase.

At dinner Tina asked about the album. Curiosity was her nature. Curiosity, whimsy. She asked about everything: why boats were only for water, why grapefruit wasn't grape, why chickens didn't just fly away.

Loren and Betty, they were told, were their great-great-grandparents. Bernie was their great-uncle. Lucille their great-grandmother—Beck's grandmother.

Beck wasn't surprised by Tina's questions, but he was surprised by the album. He hadn't seen it in years. Asked her where she found it. No one remembered putting it under the bed.

He marveled, discomfort threading his voice, at how much junk they had. Small piles like little cysts on every surface. Piles upon piles. Glancing around the dining room, the living room, he seemed fearful that more lay hidden, more would be discovered. "It's everywhere," he said.

ॐ

Day by day the cabin becomes a home. Siding goes up. Insulation. Dry-food cellar. Well pump. Windows. Loren and Betty labor dawn until dusk, perpetually tired but never tiring.

Even after the wood-burning stove is installed, the family cooks and eats most evenings around the campfire. Beans, sausage, pasties, chili, stew.

Lucille asks, "Why do we have a fire every night?"

"Fire's good company," Loren says.

Lucille considers this, then adds, "We're company too."

Her mother's smile flickers above the blaze. A light drizzle is beginning to fall. A melody of scattered raindrops plinks on a wheelbarrow.

"You're right," Loren says, voice heavy and smooth as a lake. "But we're here because of the fire. Wouldn't be alive without it."

A whistle glides in from the blackness: distant, melancholy.

Bernie and Lucille look at each other across the flames. Burning wood pops.

"Think someone's out there?" Lucille asks.

"Owl, loon, coyote, tree frog," Loren recites like a prayer. With a stick he flips a log, churns a swirl of sparks.

"Spirit," Betty says. "Spirit don't care if it makes sense to us. Just goes about its business." She sips her coffee. "Won't hurt you," she assures Lucille.

"How you know, Ma?"

"She don't know." Loren shifts on his chair, grimaces. "Don't nobody know. Them woods go dark for a reason. Best not ask."

Betty snorts but doesn't speak.

Bernie squeezes a smile. Lucille tosses a twig to keep him quiet.

❧

Beck tells a story:

"My grandmother Lucille died many years ago. I got this album after she passed on. This is important: My father wasn't given these photos even though he was Lucille's only child. She left it to me in her will. That probably pissed my father off. He never mentioned it, though. He won't admit pain, not ever.

"It's okay, Mallory, the girls can hear this. This doesn't mean I don't love your grandpa. He's just a different kind of man than me. Our values don't exactly line up.

"Lucille left nothing else to me. Just these pictures. Of course I was only fourteen. Any money she had, not that she had any, was left to my father. Her possessions were put up at an estate sale because my father said it was all trash.

"Your grandpa was unemotional about her death. I remember when he told me. One night he was putting me to bed. He never put me to bed. If anybody put me to bed it was my mother, but neither of them did it often. Tucking in, singing songs, saying good night—your grandparents didn't do that stuff.

"So it was weird for my father to come to my room. He wasn't stressed or upset. He stood there brushing dust off my dresser, absentmindedly glancing at his fingertips as he did it. He had a look on his face like he was remembering an amusing story. Then he said, 'My mother died today, or maybe last week. They aren't sure. We'll have to take you out of school for the funeral.' Then he shut off the light."

"Maybe he didn't love her," Tina said. She thought she was making a joke. Because who didn't love their mom?

Beck weighed the idea and did not disagree. "He's not an expressive man." He sipped his whiskey. Mallory pondered her lap, where her hands were occupied knitting a scarf.

"Lucille had a brother named Bernie," Beck continued. "The boy in the overalls. Your great uncle. She and Bernie grew up in a cabin. Way out in the woods. That's

Loren and Betty right there. They built that cabin from the ground up, and I mean designed it, chopped the trees, cleared the plot, dug a well, everything. Raised a tool shed, outhouse, pole barn."

As he spoke Beck's watery eyes acquired a kind of feverish sadness, or reflectiveness, as if each word was inflicting pain that he was in no hurry to relinquish. His thumb stroked the rim of his glass like a talisman.

"Took five years. Think of that. After they finished, Loren lay down in bed and slept for seventeen days. Then he was dead."

"How do you know all this stuff?" Lucy asked. She'd been listening while scrolling through texts.

Beck paused, thoughtful. With surprise he said, "I don't know."

"Family stories," Mallory offered. "You pick them up along the way. Like you girls are doing now."

"Betty lived at the cabin for another forty years after Loren died," Beck continued. "Cut her own firewood, raised chickens, shot deer."

Tina said, "What about Bernie and Lucille?"

"Bernie, well..." Beck breathed deep and slow. The whiskey seemed to be sedating him. "Might as well tell them now."

Their mother gave a somber nod.

"Your great-grandma Lucille. She killed Bernie. On accident."

Tina put her hand over her mouth. Lucy was about to reach across the couch and offer a reassuring pat when Tina giggled softly. Their parents didn't seem to hear.

"An axe. Probably they were splitting logs or messing around in the woods." He shrugged. "These things happen, but it's very sad. Terrible."

"A dreadful axe-ident," Tina said.

Lucy chuckled in spite of herself.

The girl wasn't done: "Great-grandma is an axe murderer!"

Mallory stopped knitting. "Tina."

"Who owns the place now?" Lucy asked.

Looking back, Lucy realizes she wasn't even curious. She only wanted to change the subject. Only wanted to stop thinking about an axe splitting that boy open, that boy with the crooked hair and lost eyes. Lucy would later blame herself for planting the idea in her father's head. Planting it like an axe.

"Who owns the place now?"

A simple question.

Right away she saw the flare in her father's eye, his thoughts beginning to smolder.

Stupid, stupid, stupid.

ও

"The forest wears perfume. You've smelled it: sun-baked pine, heady as fresh bread. Forest dresses stout in summer, all kinds of layers. Then she strips naked in winter—the opposite of people. Forest sings and sighs, moans and hums. Voices legion, connected millions: leaves in windblown tremble; gray-brown trunks hushed as soldiers, some kissed by sun, some drowned in shadow; rainwhisper and thunderbowl.

"The death under our feet is not death. The oak that falls in riot, compelling birds heavenward, will soften. Her trunk unstiffens and hollows. Mushrooms rise like teeth on her skin. Grubs and snakes will congregate and propagate. Descendants of descendants. No wasted. No tragic. No sadness nor tears."

Betty spoke as Lucille cradled Bernie's head in her lap.

ও

1910:

How old were Bernie and Lucille?

Sixteen and fourteen, respectively.

What did Bernie look like?

Bernie a not-so-tall young man. Packed and knotty like a bag of potatoes. Fingers thick as tow ropes and a jaw that could chew dried corn. Air drawn through parted lips, typically.

And Lucille?

A lean girl, angular with pubescence. A gap-toothed grin, hair uncombed and straight as curtains draping her chest. Muscular legs, coyote speed. Hands large as her brother's.

School?

They walked to a one-room four miles distant. On winter days they left and returned in darkness.

Both?

Only Lucille had school in 1910.

Bernie dropped out of eighth grade so he could help his mother when Pa died. Most quit anyway, especially boys. No point in more learning.

Ma didn't need help but didn't say no. Bernie could pump water, shoot a rifle, split wood, start a fire, follow directions. He was best given simple tasks. Taskless, he took up mischief.

1908:

Bernie changed after Loren died.

He'd always been streaked by troublemaking. Mostly harmless like frog-killing or locking Lucille in the tool shed. Never was a sweetheart but he could look people in the eye. Sometimes smiled with kindness.

Pa's death meant even frowning got lost or forgotten. Neutral face is what he wore.

❧

Tina pounded until Lucy opened the bathroom door.

"Quiet," Lucy said. She was applying makeup, bending so close to the mirror it felt like she might fall in.

Tina's succinct and absurdly quiet tinkle made Lucy smile. Something heartbreaking about the smallness.

"Why the fancy face?"

Lucy weighed her options. Realized they were exceptionally light. "I'm going to a dance."

"What dance?" Tina was wiping.

"Fall something-or-other. At the high school."

"Mom's frying up the fish we caught. You can't go."

"Not tonight. Two weeks."

"You're getting dressed *now*?"

Lucy laughed. "Test run." She scooted so Tina could wash hands, then puckered at the mirror.

"Are you going with a boy?"

"Mm-hmm."

"Who?"

"Shhh, Mom's in the kitchen."

"Is it a secret?"

Lucy turned one way then another, sizing up the job. Not bad. She'd never considered herself pretty but liked her eyes. Oily pools are what Jeremy Pritchett called them. Not the most poetic boy. But he meant dark and mysterious, wide and soulful. *Sure, all of that,* Jeremy had agreed when Lucy provided descriptors. It was the first flattering thing a boy had said about her. Two months later he confessed to making out with his dad's tennis instructor.

She scrubbed off the makeup after Tina promised not to tell.

She had met Noah online three weeks earlier. He had followed her on social media, introduced himself. A sixteen-year-old at Wolfolk High. Normal-looking kid, nothing amazing. But Lucy saw a window and intended to leap through even if it meant plummeting.

How do u know who I am? she wrote.

My mom works with your dad.

Horrified face emoji. *Did my dad set this up?* This seemed impossible and thankfully was.

My mom said you were homeschooled living out in bumfuck nowhere. More bumfuck than Wolfolk lol. Sounds lonely.

U have no idea.

That evening Lucy heard the whistler.

She was buried under covers, this place always so fucking cold, hiding the glow of her phone, messaging with this boy, this Noah who had appeared hours earlier like magic.

She wasn't ignorant of online danger—who was these days? She vetted him, cyber-stalked him, naturally. Unless some hacker had hijacked his profile or he was a psychotic con man, he was a junior at Wolfolk High. Two months from seventeen. Avid bowler and hunter. On the track team. Wore camo year-round, seemingly. Short hair like an army cut, and he had a pleasant head. No dimples, sadly. Low eyebrows shadowing brown eyes. Some kid months from being a man. In his messages he had a kind personality and knew how to make her laugh with quick, easy lines.

She didn't want Noah himself. She wanted what he could give her. He would introduce Lucy to other kids. She would get invited places. Everyone would ask her why she didn't go to the high school, and she would say, *Great question. You should ask my parents.* And then they *would* ask that question some night when they came over for dinner or maybe a sleepover, and Mom would sneak a glance at Dad, and in bed that night her parents would talk in hushed voices, and the next day they would announce YES. We were wrong. Wrong to drag you here and hide you from the world. We're meeting the principal this afternoon.

Notions like flitterflies buttering around the yard. Lucy felt happy for the first time since the move and wanted to shove the sensation into her mouth and swallow it.

She lay messaging under bedcovers. Then she heard the whistler. A seven-note melody. A minor key. Lucy had played flute for six years. At first Lucy thought it was Tina, and her reaction was to turn off her phone and feign sleep.

Then she remembered Tina couldn't whistle.

The tune came again. The same incomplete phrase begging for resolution:

E-flat up to B flat.

Down to F-sharp, then F.

Up to C-sharp, down to C, down to G-sharp.

She envisioned the quarter-notes in her head. Wondered if she had imagined them. Wondered if she'd heard them every night but never noticed

The whistle came a third time. A whiteness opened inside her and spread through her veins. Breathless, she couldn't move.

One more whistle and she would run to her parents' room. Run like a child. Beg them to either shove her outside into the dark woods half-naked, lock the door, and never let her back in; or to bring her into their bed, hold her, protect her—and maybe these two were the same thing.

❧

"You can't keep him in here," Lucille said.

"Got air holes, food, water. What else he need?"

"To be outside."

"He ain't a normal rabbit."

The box was open. The rabbit showed no desire to flee. He wasn't injured or old, simply preferred sitting and watching to moving. Seemed to apprehend that freedom would arrive in good time or perhaps even burgeon within this crude crate.

Lucille and Bernie crouched in black pine shadow. A dry leaf skittered across the dirt like an animal rushing to attack. The sun had been consumed by a swift gray cloud, and now the wind bit hard. Days could be warm and blue and then tumble fifteen sudden degrees.

"It's okay," Bernie said, sensing Lucille's worry about getting caught in the rain. "We ain't far. If there's lightning I'll put you in my pocket, little sister." Sometimes he was cruel, other times he doted. He changed fast as weather.

Lucille wanted to see the rabbit's teeth but was afraid. Scared it was true they were human. Anyway, the rabbit wouldn't let her look. Kept its head low and wasn't mean but wasn't friendly either. Bernie said it was a boy, but how did Bernie know? He never lifted it up to prove it, so Lucille thought of the creature as a sexless thing like a tree or cloud.

It had the softest fur she ever felt. The deepest burnt-log eyes. Bernie seemed to never touch or look at it. She wondered how the animal had such a hold on him. Wondered if the rabbit was keeping Bernie instead of the other way around.

She swatted at mosquitoes singing in her ear. For three days the rabbit had been in the box and she hadn't heard it whistle. She was sure Bernie had made it up like the human teeth.

He made up lots, especially with Pa sick in bed for two weeks. Bernie hated school, played hooky whenever he could, got in trouble. Stole erasers from the teacher's desk. Pinned a boy face down in the schoolyard and fed him worms. Probably wanted to get kicked out. Now with Pa bedridden and Ma caregiving and hunting and everything else, Bernie acted up even more.

Not that Pa had ever been around. He mostly showed attention by laying on them with a belt or stick or anything handy. Never angry whipping, just discipline. Claimed it was love that swung the switch. When he was drunk he got soft and thoughtful and shared quiet conversation. Lucille liked him best full of whiskey.

"Pa didn't go to school," Bernie would say. Ma couldn't disagree and couldn't name a reason her boy should finish.

He was practically begging to get expelled, and some of that delinquency snuck home. Still he was a good brother and couldn't be blamed for being simple. Maybe for wanting to stay simple, Lucille thought. She never spoke this aloud.

"He'll whistle for you someday." Bernie touched her shoulder though she didn't require comfort. His arm around her, she breathed his body. "He whistles when death is coming."

Lucille pictured their pa feverish beneath the quilt. The stench from that room was invisible horror.

She felt a sudden need to shut him up. There was no death in the air. Bernie was a liar and a simpleton. "What about when we was at the camp fire? Pa wasn't sick then."

"Funny you ask." His sidelong glare challenged her. "Day after, that hunter got shot out by the creek."

"That was day before."

"After. Bet."

She wanted to bet but usually lost. Bernie kept his hand extended until it was clear she wasn't biting.

Their mother's voice broke the quiet. The wind was cold, the trees bowing. Ma's tone, shrill and urgent, rode the breeze. Bernie and Lucille scampered through twilight and brush, rain beginning to fall.

Halfway home they heard the whistle behind them, pursuing: a simple seven-note melody.

When they got to the cabin Pa was a branch.

"Your application is something else," Alaina said.

Her office was basically a closet tucked in the rear of a storage room where inventory filled dusty shelves. The drop ceiling had been removed. Exposed pipes gurgled above their heads. On Alaina's desk, manila folders and order forms were crooked heaps deficient of structural integrity.

Beck sat sideways so his knees didn't jam against the desk. The room was grossly hot. His jacket and tie— overkill, he knew—made breathing a chore. But something had shifted in him once he decided to make this move. He was a different person or wanted to be. One aspect he was determined to change was doing things half-cocked, sitting back and letting life happen, letting his father happen. A pricey suit chosen and purchased by himself symbolized initiative, misguided or not.

Eponymous Alaina coughed like cracked kindling and set flame to a cigarette. She was a senior with tightly permed hair, inexplicably blond. Bright white dentures crammed her mouth. With a finger-lick she flipped to page 2 of his application. Beck suspected she might live

150 years. This kind of woman had been elderly since age forty. Unlike Beck's father, this woman embraced the passage of time. He could tell by looking at her. Probably bore her first child at eighteen, a grandmother by thirty-six.

He wasn't judging; this was how people lived out here. *How people lived*—what did he mean by that? *Out here.*

Admit it, he told himself, they're hicks to you. Yes, he admitted it. And he wanted to be one of them. Or be near them, anyway. Their lives were uncomplicated. They didn't have much, didn't need much, and this earned Beck's admiration. His whole spoiled life had been gifted to him. Brand-name clothes, a sprawling house, a designer bathroom meant success.

Alaina tapped her cigarette on the ashtray. "You really got a master's degree from MIT?" Daughter of a farmer, maybe. Pipefitter. Assembly line worker. Born into blissful wanting.

"Correct," he said.

"No offense, but why the hell you want to work here?"

Beck considered the question. He had approached every Wolfolk business that would accept an application: dry cleaner, gas station, hardware store, jerky processor, tavern. Alaina's was the first and only to offer an interview.

"I need to support my family," he said. It was the truth.

"Sweetie, this is a fry cook position." She removed her glasses as if to see him better, and her warm old rubbery face flashed a cautioning smile. "You're gonna make a quarter of what you're used to."

"I'll work the shit shifts. Holidays, nights, weekends. I'll bus tables, wash dishes, clean toilets. I want to get dirty."

Afterward Beck stepped onto the sidewalk of the main street. Above the church a flock of birds curled toward the sunset—a circle bending, dispersing, and re-forming as if bound by unseen thread. Beck let the warm summer breeze fill him. He loosened his tie as he walked to the car. *My car*, he thought with a bitter smile, turning the phrase in his head while climbing in.

At the wheel he sat. Breathed the stale fabric. He tilted the rearview mirror and stared into his eyes. Same color as his father's. Same eyebrows, jowls. He was transforming, something he hoped would never happen. He assumed his father's clipped delivery: "Now, Beck, you realize what you're doing, don't you? You're on the fast-track to failure and I would be remiss if I didn't speak up. You hear me? You should really take a breath on this one, shouldn't you? I don't want to see you fall on your face again."

Beck started the engine and decided to find the nearest car dealer. Trade this thing in for a goddamn pickup.

❧

October 1, 2007:

I'm better at my obituary than my diary. The obituary was fun. This is hard.

Mom is making me do this. Teacher mom, not mom-mom, although they look alike. She says I should write every day.

My problem is audience and reason. I can't write to no one for nothing. That's like screaming into a well.

So I'm writing to you. Can I call you Lucille? It's a penful to write *Great-Grandma* every time.

I'll introduce myself. My name is Christina Monarch Randall, and I'm thirteen. My words are flying through the portal of time—back, back, one hundred years, a perfect round century. Picture a calendar flipping and spinning and getting sucked into black. All the way to you.

You never got married, did you? I just realized you have the same last name as my dad, so I guess something happened with you and your husband. I don't think women in your time kept their birth names. Did they? I'll need to get to the bottom of this mystery.

I'm not here to pry or get personal. I'm doing this for school, which happens to be my home. Did you go to school? We're living at the same place you lived, did you know that? The cabin your mom and dad built. They did an amazing job. We had to redo most of it because the forest was trying to eat it, but everything looks modern now. Same bones, fresh skin. I'm trying to figure out how you got to school if you did go to school. Ride a horse? Swing from vines? I don't think cars were invented then but maybe. Another research topic. It would be a long walk and I think you had no wings nor school bus.

My middle name isn't Monarch. I just like that word. It's Tina Elizabeth Randall. When I'm legal I'll change it. Maybe I'll even ditch Tina, become someone new.

These woods are like a person. Some days calm and happy, some days hot and mean. Also soggy and sad. When I see a blackbird or squirrel or deer I think they're relatives of the same animals you saw. Their blood is *their* blood, like yours is mine. You're inside me and my sister and my dad.

And now my reason: I'm making a formal inquiry about death. Does it hurt? Is it real? Is it the end of everything or the beginning? Don't answer now. Take your time. We'll talk about it when you're ready.

I'm hungry for lunch. We don't kill deer like your family probably did. Dad wants to but he doesn't know how (don't tell him I said this). We eat salami. Goodbye.

The earth fought against them. The forest did not want this realignment, these cuts and amendments. It garnered forces to drive them away: snow, rain, ice, and wind; sickness and hunger; scourge of wasps, horse-flies, and mosquitoes.

Betty, bless her. Too good for him. A mother unconditionally albeit unemotionally, but a worker besting even most men he knew. Mute and tireless as a mule. Her passion was laying hand to soil. Skin blistered by hammer and heat with no complaint. No fear of sun or dark or beast.

Loren was born into bloodshed, a child of the Civil War, his father a soldier in the Union army shot in a field when Loren was barely weaned. His mother cared for Loren and his three brothers, but they were poor as Job's turkey. A monthly pittance from the government was what her husband's life was worth. The brothers stole apples, potatoes, and beans from nearby farms until the oldest took buckshot to the right leg and could never move well after that. Loren the youngest, called *baby boy* even into his teenage years, felt trapped in their Saginaw home. His brothers were laborers, his mother perpetually ill. Life looked to be a tedious death. Loren at age seventeen set off on his own and always regretted not being with his ma when she died two months later.

He walked and hitched wagon rides, aiming for the Lake Michigan shore. Never made it. In a town of fifty-six named Blessing he met Betty. He'd been doing odd jobs for whoever was hiring, years rootless and unsettled. He was paid to paint the barn in this particular case. Betty was the farmer's daughter, a humorless girl not so much sightly as compelling. Mystery behind her eyes, she would watch from the front porch as he perspired in the sun. He slept fitfully in the barn each night, breathed manure from neighboring cattle farms, and on the fifth day gestured for her to come talk to him.

She shunned dresses unlike most young ladies. Overalls. Long hair braided behind her head as if showing off her face. Up close he saw how pretty she was in a masculine way, her expression that said don't trifle and if you would like to speak to me you need to make me want to listen. Wide eyes the color of wet straw, she enjoyed buttermilk and whittling animals with a hunting blade. Bears and horses mostly, though he requested a dog and she complied. It looked pretty much like a bear but Loren swore otherwise.

They were married a month later and lived in the attic room in her family home. Betty bore a son and then a daughter. Father wanted Betty and Loren to stay and work the farm, but Betty had brothers and another sister, and she was the eldest and first to be married. She deserved a chance to make her own way.

They headed west on the same highway Loren had originally tread. This time with a small wagon, one horse, and two babies. Loren had saved a good bit of money. They stayed with a colony of Quakers for a while raising barns and homes. Their hosts' religion the Randalls kept a distance from, but the Quakers fed them and paid decent wages.

Loren was a drinker from age fifteen. No exception with the Quakers. He hid it best he could and never let it affect his work until the trouble.

He sank deep after what that man done to Bernie. The unspeakable thing. The vileness that created visions. Loren drank more, more often. Betty took to banging pans to rouse him. His face lost its light. His tongue lost its sweetness. His measurements went crooked.

When the Quakers said they would cure that man

with prayer and Bible instead of law, neither Loren nor Betty would have it. Upon this he and Betty agreed: God did not factor into their lives. He may have created the heavens and earth but after that His involvement was unreliable and puzzling.

Neither Betty nor Loren ever discussed what Loren did next, the reason they packed their belongings and fled the Quakers in the moonless night. One minute their life was here; the next they were homeless and watching over their shoulders.

What Betty and Loren had learned about construction they decided to put to their own use. Loren heard about a plot for cheap near Wolfolk. Acreage wild and untamed, the seller warned. Land that God forgot. Betty and Loren said it sounded perfect.

❧

Noah wanted to meet. Lucy wanted the same. But how, how?

From one moment to the next her strategy shifted. First she pondered honesty because was it a crime to meet a person? A sin to flee the compound for a few hours?

But she foresaw the drama. Dad cinching his mouth, disapproval leaking from his pores. Mom the peace-maker offering stale compromise: *Why don't you have this young man over for lunch? You could show him the woods.* Show him the woods like he'd never seen it. Even at their home in the city her parents hadn't allowed her to go out with boys. Meeting Noah for the first time under the eyes of her parents, in this tiny place, nowhere to go, nowhere to hide. Nightmare.

She mulled deception. She could invent a reason to leave. A lie but more of a fib. For days she was distracted from lessons and assignments, pondering possibilities. None would fly:

Some of my old Norrix friends are coming to town! They want to meet in Wolfolk and have coffee.

Why don't you tell them to come to the cabin? You can show them the woods.

(And where would someone have coffee in Wolfolk anyway? At Alaina's FAMILY RESTAURANT?)

I need time to myself. I'm going to walk into town for the day.

(To most parents a reasonable request. Not hers. They would insist: too far, too buggy, too dangerous, too too too. They hadn't even let Lucy take driver's training because what's the rush?)

I want to apply for a part-time job. You don't need a job.

There's a used flute on Craigslist I want to go look at. You don't play the flute anymore.

I need to go into town and murder everyone who reminds me of you. Great, we'll drive you.

She couldn't tell them about Noah. The feces would rain, the quiet shit-storm that drowned you. Her parents never got mad; they glummed, they guilted. They treated with silence. Her dad claimed to be relaxed, easy-going, hey, to each their own! Meanwhile his face screamed *disappointed*.

What did her parents expect? Lock up a young lady and she'll be a happy captive?

The more Lucy thought, the more she blamed them. No sane person would tolerate this life.

Finally she settled on a particular deception: just sneak the fuck out.

Easier said than done. It would have to be late at night. When Beck closed the restaurant he didn't get home until two a.m. Mom and Tina went to bed at ten. When not working, her father stayed up until midnight.

Noah said he would park halfway up their two-mile seasick driveway. I'll be waiting in my car, he said. Lights off so nobody will notice.

He couldn't wait to see her in person. They could drive into town, do whatever. She would be home before sunrise.

The threads they touch my head.

Especially when I'm in bed.

I think about you dead.

❧

All the windblown misery ends up here. Betty sensed it as soon as they began clearing the land. The feeling was intangible yet palpable, a pollen on the breeze that sowed images as she slept: a silk scarf stretched over an infant's face until the nursling expired; a wizened chalky woman in a Sunday dress reposing in an open grave. Newness and rot, horror and beauty fused.

The clearing had created a stage for nature's dramaturgy. Not a frightening feeling; factual and—to Betty's sense—inevitable, as if she were merely being shown the rules out here. She was unnerved by the visions but considered humans a part of the natural world no different than wolf or badger, not superior as the Bible argued nor inferior. She did not think this move a mistake nor wrought with danger. Aside from the expected challenges of surviving off the land, they would need to accommodate is all, be mindful of the system they were intruding upon.

Still, she wondered about the power of the Quaker prayers. In sleep sometimes she saw that man and his blood-caved face, his barren socket, and worried that the Quakers had invoked divine forces to pursue and punish.

Her father had devoted his life to studying the land, coaxing it, working it into a shape he could profit from, balancing respect with need and purpose. From the Indians he had learned a great deal about harmony with the natural world.

But he felt it too, the windblown misery. Betty had written him after she and Loren purchased the property. Her family rode fifty miles in a horse-drawn wagon to visit. For a week they camped, helped out with Bernie and Lucille, felled trees, dug the well, pitched in however they could. Their company was a benediction, although Loren and Betty did not use such a word; privately, Betty felt nourished and provided for.

"Don't fight what's given," her father said. He had aged since she last saw him, white hair wispy and hands crimping from arthritis. The bottle was handed to him and he swigged and passed it.

"It's harsh land," Betty said, as if he couldn't see it himself. She wanted confirmation, maybe even a reason to abandon the project. But Loren had never wavered, and neither should she.

Her father nodded, eyes campfire yellow. The wind blew smoke into Betty's face. She shielded herself, and when the air cleared she looked up to see tears on her father's cheeks. He had never cried in front of her.

"No such thing as gentle land," he whispered. She strained to hear him. Everyone else was talking, laughing, dancing. Her brother Robert played the fiddle.

"No pleasure knowing we're all to die," he continued, surveying his family. "But sometimes death isn't death, and life isn't life. The two get mixed and turned."

He wasn't drunk, although Loren was, and Betty could see her husband across the fire, tilted and fading against a pile of lumber, cigarette lazy in his lips, long past useful.

"You just have to recognize when one is the other," he said. "And plan accordingly." He was giving a warning or a command or both, but Betty's mind was too fogged by exhaustion and drink to know.

She touched her father's hand. His skin was warm and dry. She hadn't spoken to him in five years.

The week passed with campfires, friendship, and merriment. In her previous life at home they had never gotten along so well. The windblown misery bonded them against the dark, or so it seemed. It felt like a good omen.

When the week expired her family mounted their buckboard, proceeded slow and precarious along the narrow way into the forest, and never returned.

What treasures did you seek? Did you want a clear path for fire on your lips? Did you get the scream of flame to usher you to the other side?

No treasure without if not within.

They speak while Lucy sleeps. I sneak into the dark without shoes.

Loren blended with the sheets as if he was becoming them. His eyes were holes, his breath a gasp. The doctor on the tenth day stood bedside and pronounced pneumonia.

Lucille heard three words, a question: *New moan, ya?*

Her father moaned often, so the question felt true. Lucille thought of a new moon. New moon. New moan. New morn'. New man.

Loren was a different person under the sickness. Weak, hot-faced, lost, he ranted in fever dreams that the forest was a dance, the cabin a fortress against. In a rasp he mumbled outlandishly: up and down united, soil and clouds bound by pulses of birdwing and frog croak, tree veins extracting water to the branchfingers. Blood from the sky, disease in the blood. Drowned moon in the pond, reborn moon in the heavens; both unreachable and forever.

Betty told his children he would be gone soon. She asked them to hold his hand so he could carry their faces to the other side. The other side of what was Lucille's question, although she knew the answer. Not heaven, not hell; she did not credit these places. Her parents did not believe these myths. Bernie accepted them because he swallowed simple stories like candy. Lucille despite being younger had vision, could read the stitched shadows, the poetry of moonlight sketching truth beyond language upon the pine needles. Lucille felt tremors where she walked, knowing she was the uninvited. She the visitor. She the hairless and toothless with no defense. She the forest food.

The reason animal feared man had none to do with original sin or threat. A person could hurt the earth no more than a hairpin could stab the sun.

The animals' fear had everything to do with the impossibility of tears and laughter.

❧

The heads they touch my tread. Your tread is red
Under the storm cloud.

❧

Friday in mid-October, moments past midnight:

Lucy climbed from sleep. Found her father as usual on the sofa with his glass. TV muted, an action scene, bullets and cars. Father stone-faced. No light but the screen flicker.

"My stomach hurts," she said when Beck turned.

"Ginger ale," he muttered, ice clinking. "In the pantry maybe."

His voice was like butter on a stove, meaning he might be soon for bed. She hoped. She went to the bathroom and found the makeup bag she'd stashed behind the first aid kit.

When she opened the door fifteen minutes later he was standing there.

"Jesus, Dad."

He leaned in to study her face. She shut off the light.

"Feeling better?"

"Mostly," she said.

"Are you wearing makeup?"

"Of course not." She ducked under his arm and went into the kitchen. At the sink she poured a glass of water. Pulse hammering.

Her dad followed. He set his glass on the counter, then his hand on the back of her neck. She shivered from his cold fingers. "You look nice," he said. "You're allowed to be whoever you want to be."

She shrugged him off and headed toward her room. "I'm not wearing makeup, Dad. You're drunk."

She closed the bedroom door. She heard him chuckling.

For thirty, forty, fifty minutes she stared at the null

gray ceiling. She could still feel his fingers, a residual chill. He almost never touched her or Tina. Even their mother. Displays of affection were not his thing. She guessed this was an awkward attempt to redefine himself, a goal she'd overheard him talking about with her mom. She wondered if heavy drinking was also part of the plan. Since the move he put away half a bottle of whiskey each night.

When she was sure he was in bed she crawled from the covers. Tina the Queen lay sideways, one foot dangling off the mattress. A bizarre sleeper but a heavy one. Still, Lucy would proceed with care.

She dressed in the dark, having assembled an outfit in the bottom drawer of her dresser. She unplugged phone from charger, slid it into her purse.

Outside, the air was cool. Arms crossed, she hugged herself. The wind exhaled all around but she didn't feel it. Here she was sheltered by trees. She'd never ventured into the woods at night, and as the path snaked deeper and the porch light faded, she felt nervous. A dim moon winked under clouds. Her cell flashlight cast a puny glow onto the dirt; bugs swarmed. She shut off the light and let her eyes acclimate.

Maybe he wouldn't show. Now, in the naked woods, her plan seemed foolish. To meet a stranger in this blackness under the eyes of no one—was she so stupid? Emotions had clouded her judgment. She'd been desperate, so lonely and angry. This was a mistake.

But she didn't stop walking. Didn't or couldn't. Each step ushered her further from reality, her breath a curling vapor dissipating like a dream. Night was a playground for hunters, for the haunted lightless past. Her fear mounted, weighting her steps. She could return to her warm comforter. It would be so easy.

Then she saw Beck and his whiskey, Mallory's unthinking smile. She forged ahead until not far away an unfocused shape emerged, a shadowy bulk in the path.

A car. Excitement threaded her fear.

A man was leaning against the car. Looking at her. She stopped fifty paces distant. She would not call out. Her body braced to flee.

Then a light came alive in the man's hand. A phone. A face appeared, and it was Noah.

"Jesus," she said. She closed the gap, cautiously glancing into the car—maybe he'd brought friends, a gang, a gang rape. She shook the image from her mind as she reached him. "Usually guys wait a month before they turn creepy."

He turned a flashlight, a powerful beam, to his face as if to convince her further of his identity. "We work quick out here," he said.

They shook hands. To Lucy it seemed the wrong

custom, too formal for teenagers on a dirt drive at one in the morning. But his grip felt nice. She let it linger. She realized she hadn't touched anyone in a long time—Father's ghost fingers on her neck—and twice in the same night seemed more than coincidental.

"Now what?" she asked.

"Got a six-pack of Coors and a tank of gas."

"Classy."

"Got a better idea?"

"Plenty, but most of them involve being reborn as a different person."

"One of my main talents is cruising. Which is good luck for you since it's the only thing to do around here."

"Maybe we could just get in your car? These fucking mosquitoes." She slapped her cheek where one had lighted.

They climbed into the front seat. He used a lighter to open two bottles.

"Sorry it's not cold."

"You went all out."

"Nothing too good for the daughter of a fry cook," he said.

"He's not a fry cook."

"He just plays one on TV."

"He's just an idiot."

"Harsh."

Lucy swigged the beer, the bottle warm and solid in her hand.

"I heard he's an electrical engineer? My mom was laughing about it, saying the economy must really be in the shitter."

"Something's in the shitter," Lucy said.

"So he really wanted to be a fry cook?" She could smell his cologne. His profile was good-looking. Hair freshly cut.

"Who knows. He wants to prove he's a man. It's like he's dragging us all along for his mid life crisis. Do you smoke?"

He nodded at the glove compartment. She brought out the pack and they each lit a cigarette.

"Need to crack the windows," he said, turning the key halfway. "So you're using me to get back at the old man." He chuckled, an odd quiet puff. "I'm okay with that."

They smoked and drank. Lucy felt like she was inside a protective chamber, a hermetically sealed bubble where she could finally breathe, finally speak. She wanted to bitch about loss, about lonely, about bored, about stir-crazy—but she realized with regret that she'd already said most of this in her DMs. Her head buzzed.

"You're even prettier in person," he said. His cigarette he slipped out the window. She took a last drag—

the taste was terrible but amazing—and followed his lead. He scooted closer and politely took her beer and set it in the cup holder.

"You're not so bad yourself."

His hand was strong, vivid, bones and flesh, hard and soft coexistent.

He kissed her and she kissed him back, their breathing fast and shallow. Each gripped the other like the moment couldn't be lost if they held tight. Her lips found his neck, which tasted like musk and salt, his cologne an unbearable flower. Her eyelids fluttered, little bird wings, as his hands wandered her thighs.

After a few moments they parted, panting and embarrassed. Noah blew out a long breath. "Damn, girl," he said.

"Damn yourself."

He turned the key halfway to get the blowers going. The windows were white. They defogged with their sleeves.

Lucy screamed.

"Jesus, what?"

"A girl."

"Where?"

"Out there, out there." Lucy leaned across the seat, seeking the headlights.

"I got it."

Beams exploded the darkness, exposing the world as inelegant and without mystery: dirt drive, trees, low weeds lining.

"I don't see anything." He shut off the lights.

"I think it was my sister."

He put a hand on Lucy's arm; she was gripping the door handle. "Hang on," he said. "I'll drive you."

"I need to go. I need to see if it was Tina."

"I'll come."

She opened the door. "I'll text you when I get home." She mustered a smile despite the uneasiness. "I had a good time."

"I don't feel right about you wandering these woods."

"I'm not even sure what I saw. Probably just a weird tree."

"Then stay."

"The dance is in two weeks. We need to figure out how to make that happen."

She blew him a kiss. He didn't catch it.

When she reached the cabin, the side door stood partially open. She gripped her keychain mace as she entered. As if mace would help. As if she could fight off a wolf or an axe murderer. Or a goddamn raccoon. Flipping on kitchen lights, any lights, would have been a good option under normal circumstances, but the last thing she needed was her parents finding her stinking of booze and smoke.

Had Tina been out there in the woods? Had the twerp really followed her?

Lucy closed the door, locked it, and slipped off her shoes. In the kitchen nothing appeared out of place. Living room: unmolested. No hidden burglars, seemingly.

She drew a long breath and entered the bedroom.

Eyes closed, blankets pulled to her chin: Tina.

❧

My head is dead.

❧

In the morning Lucille and Ma walked to a clearing fifty feet beyond the tool shed. Betty carried shovel and pick, Lucille a shovel and canteen. Betty measured using heel-to-toe, dragging the pick to mark the edges.

The summer soil gave way without resistance. For hours they dug in the heat. Bernie had stayed inside with the body. Said he wanted time alone with his father. Said he would clean and dress him. Her son's washed-out expression, as if someone had removed his eyes and wrung the color before shoving them back in, convinced Betty not to argue. She and the girl could fashion the grave.

"How deep, Ma?"

With a forearm Betty wiped her head. Her dirt-caked fingers were like roots pulled from the earth. "Needs a lot on top of him, this one," she said. "He did not want to leave and might be tempted to return if the load ain't heavy."

They dug until the hole stood chest deep. Lucille's shoulders burned. Her stomach growled from hunger, though the thought of food made her queasy. She drank the last of the water from the canteen. Betty stuck her vegetable fingers in her mouth and whistled. "Make room for Daddy," she said. Lucille climbed out of the grave.

Bernie emerged from the cabin dragging a rolled blanket with their father inside. He wouldn't look up. Lucille suspected her brother was ashamed of his earlier emotions. Now, however, instead of shock or sadness, a blade glinted in his eyes. His wan face churned and nostrils flared as he strained against the corpse's weight. Betty watched her boy like a mother watching her baby's first steps. As if she expected him to fall and wouldn't move to stop it. As if in the long run falling was best.

When Lucille stepped forward to help, Betty shook her head. The women watched as Bernie sat on the soil and pulled his father into an awkward embrace near the edge of the pit. He panted scornful fire as sweat streamed his face. With a curl of his body Bernie wrenched and let gravity seize the dead; it thudded into the pit, blanket and all.

"You fucker," Bernie hissed. "You deserved it." He spat into the hole and kicked the mound, showering dirt. "Get under, get under!"

Betty tried to drag him away, but he twisted free. Rage tremored his hands and face. Lucille did not know what to do, did not understand what possessed him. When Bernie fiddled with his trousers to unbutton his fly, Betty slapped his cheeks one after the other. He ran into the woods cursing her and didn't return for three days.

Whisper claws murmuring on the door. Scratching. *Let me in.* Insistent. Lucy would not open the door. She knew what waited out there. Death. Horror. Unlove and pain.

Go away. Go away. Go away.

Lucy woke to her own gasping. Sunlight filled the window. Tina was humming a nursery-school song while sketching in bed.

Lucy closed her eyes. Not ready. "Can't you do that somewhere else?" Her jaw was sore as if she'd been grinding her teeth.

"I was trying to wake you up," Tina said.

Breathe in, breathe out. So close to sleep. The scratch of Tina's charcoal pencil. The return of the humming.

"Get out of here."

"I have to correct you," Tina said.

Lucy chose not to answer.

"It's my job as your sister."

"Fuck off."

"As you wish."

Lucy heard Tina climb out of bed. Heard feet padding the floor like a bird pecking a spongy tree. Tina closed the latch as if trying not to wake her. Little bitch. So she'd actually been there, a mile into the woods, the middle of night, to spy on her.

And Lucy had been stupid enough to tell her about the dance. She kicked off her covers. The clock read 8:05.

After getting dressed Lucy saw the open sketch pad on Tina's bed.

A drawing of a rabbit. Solid black, shaded thick. Smiling with white human teeth.

Saturdays were worse than schooldays. Nothing but sit around and drink coffee and lose your mind. Dream about a world beyond the trees. Remember skate parks, restaurants, freedom. Even homework felt like escape.

Today was worse than usual. Stale taste of cigarettes. Mild beer headache. Not enough sleep and the relentless perky moon of Tina orbiting. Lucy, lodged on the sofa, didn't want to talk or listen. Earbuds in, she slaved at an essay for her mom's version of English class, which more accurately should have been called Write Whatever Crap You Want 101.

Dad and Mom said they were going into town. Grocery day. Did the girls want to come?

Lucy prayed for Tina to say yes. She wanted to be alone. Take a nap. Masturbate, do some scream therapy. Message with Noah. Sext with Noah.

When Tina said no, Lucy's options narrowed: stay in prison with Fanciful Queen or take a three-hour trip to a not-so-super market with her parents.

A punch to the gut or a kick to the shin.

Bernie turned off. Daytime found him chair-bound on the porch, dim as a doused lamp. Sleep became his waking. As night grew and he crossed over, he stood up from bed. Up and down the creaking floor he walked. His hands gesticulated. Eyes open but unseeing he wept, cursed, laughed—alive in a world other than this.

You will be destitute by law of the pig. Bastard wood lifters. I

won't. I won't. NO! A train, Pa, a truck. Oh, this ain't special.
Haha, no. Not like an apple pie special. It smells rotten in here.
Run. Please run. We gotta go. I'm scared. The sun's underneath
us now. Where are you?

NO. Don't make me wait here. I can't feel my fingers. Please.
I'm special.

He whistles me when the wind tells him. I go out and listen.
Don't think about it, Pa. Don't think a box. My rabbit ain't in
no other box, not a box without a body. We all get a box. I want
mine mine mine.

Bernie's sentences were wild ropes that choked Lucille as she burrowed beneath her pillow. Betty lay awake in bed, listened to make sure he didn't hurt himself. Or Lucille. He remembered nothing in the morning.

He had returned after three days looking starved but clean. Told them he slept under the stars and listened to the whistler and bathed in the pond.

Betty didn't know what he meant by the whistler, so Lucille told her about the rabbit. She led her mother to the hiding spot, but box and rabbit were gone.

One day Lucille and Betty sat at the kitchen table drinking hot ginger water. Bernie chopped wood out back. Whump. Whump. Crack. Whump. Whump. Crack.

"Why's he acting like this?" Lucille asked.

In the ruddy morning light, Betty's face bore lines

Lucille had never seen. Her face had no more room. Her story was etched there, deeper now, her visage like fruit gone bad especially under the eyes.

Yet her eyes blazed blue life, which made Lucille see her ma as one of those engines, those automobiles being built downstate—you couldn't see the inside, but the machine shook and rumbled and carried you far without wearying. Faster than a horse, stronger than fifty.

"Your brother," Betty said, "might be slipping off."

"What's wrong with him?"

Betty filled her pipe from the tin. The pipe was— had been—Loren's, but Betty sometimes used it. These days used it often. "Tell you what you don't know, what I didn't ever want to tell you." She struck a match and kissed seven puffs until the air swam with sweet cherry smoke.

Betty plucked a tobacco strand from her lips, breathed like a stone skipping across water. "He was barely not a baby. Them Quakers were good to us, gave us food and work. Your pa and me helped raise barns, sheds, carriages. First the Quakers didn't want a woman working with the men, but we convinced them. Difficult labor and long days. Pay was fine, people friendly. I gave off you and your brother to a girl daytime. Maybe thirteen years old. Smart as bait but sweet. She took good care of you, you and a troupe of youngsters at her home. You don't remember, you were still a suckling. But that girl's father, well sometimes he liked to go home for lunch instead of eating on site with the other men…" Her cheek jiggled like a fishing rod getting a nibble. "Guess he was doing it to other kids too. Not just your brother. But when your pa found out he about killed himself. Went hard to the bottle, couldn't work. Showed up late or not at all. We thought police would put that man in prison. Quakers didn't report nothing. Said they followed their own law and justice. Made that man say extra prayers or who-knows-what to get squared, and I guess they figured he paid his debt. Your pa lost it. One night stumbled right over and set a brick to that man's face. Never seen ruin like that. One eye hanging. Teeth all over the floor. Didn't die. Some sort of miracle if you believe in miracles. If you believe devils find mercy." Her hand palsied as she puffed her pipe. "Had to pack up and get out fast. Quakers didn't blame your father but didn't let it pass. They're a family. Didn't matter what that devil did, they was returning the favor sometime. Not so many words that's what the elders said, and we took them serious."

"That's when we came here?"

She nodded.

"Does Bernie remember?"

The pipe cloud churned between them like a living organism. Bernie's axe thudded like a heartbeat.

"His rage against your father was rage against that man. Against your pa not protecting him."

"He was so little. He doesn't remember."

"We're same as trees, Lucille. Want to know a tree, check underground. Want to know a person, look under the soil. That's where the story is. Roots. That's what says how high, how strong, how rotten."

An enormous plastic cow head was bolted to the front of the IGA. Ten feet high and equally wide, an iconic oddity that like most things in town felt both quaint and mysterious. Mysterious as in *why*. Beck wondered at the significance of this giant cow—actually, bull was technically correct. Yet he did not wish to inquire to the owners, preferring all facets of Wolfolk at arm's length.

Mallory was in love with the head. Thought it cute and cool. Pulled out the camera each time. "How many pictures can you have?" Beck said.

"I swear it has a new expression," she said.

The Randalls bought bulk food once a month. Stocked up as much as storage space allowed. The second fridge and freezer in the pole barn helped, though Beck hated those appliances. His father had bought them, insisting Beck had no foresight. Insisting they would need to stock up if they lived on the edge of the world. Beck said no; Mallory capitulated.

Restaurant work meant Beck was known around Wolfolk. Nod to the bean farmer buying liver, nod to the woman from Friends of the Library selecting fresh buns. Introductions to Mallory, weather talk and courteous smiles. Not unpleasant nor stimulating. Tepid water, this life, and Beck guzzled it down. He was in unfamiliar territory as the face of his family, as curiosity, as standout. So accustomed to fading into the background. They loaded the pickup bed with bags. Brown paper bags! A land trapped in time.

"Shame to head back so soon," Mallory said. "Anything else we want to do?"

"Been a while since we had a liquid lunch."

"Can't stay long because of the freezer stuff." She smiled, conspiratorial. "One couldn't hurt."

The Four Star wasn't crowded. Window blinds closed, the cool half-dark of dream. Two slouched men on stools, necks bowed like water birds, gripped glasses of beer. A gray-haired couple kept wordless company in a corner booth. Above the bar a television whispered cable news, the world scrolling past.

Beck went barside and ordered a Stella Artois, which

inspired in the tender a simple head shake. Beck settled for High Life. Vodka cranberry for Mallory.

Air smoky, the couple in the corner settled under a cloud of their own making. Tin ashtrays on every table. Glass ketchup bottles and saltshakers. The Randalls felt welcomed into a world halted and unchanged. A wooden hand-carved sign: *If our prices seem expensive, keep drinking.* A scuffed linoleum floor. Mirrors of the Budweiser Beer Wolf and buxom St. Paulie Girl.

At the booth they laughed, remembering what they could about their lives before this place, before each other, before the girls. They'd been deviant college students, or so they chose to believe. Mallory played Patsy Cline on the jukebox and sang the words. They ordered another round.

The bartender came over looking like a linebacker. Tight gray T-shirt, salt-and-pepper beard. On his forearm: *death is for quitters.* "You're the cook at Alaina's, aren't you?"

"Cook is too generous," Beck said. "But I can mop floors like nobody's business." Beck and Mallory introduced themselves.

"Not many people move to Wolfolk. Most try to get away."

"We love it," Mallory said. "Such a different vibe than the city. I feel so comfortable, honestly." She was talkative when she drank. It was endearing. Beck hadn't seen it in some time.

"I heard you was living way out off 93," the bartender said. "My brother-in-law did some of your plumbing."

"Tell him he did a great job. Love those pipes," Mallory said, wearing a chuckle.

"Took a while to fix it up."

"It was a *mess*."

"Something wrong with that land," a voice said. It was the gray-haired man at the smoky booth. His face emerged from around the corner, huge black-framed glasses and a frown.

"Hush," the old lady said. She wasn't visible to Beck.

"Spooky land," the man continued. His eyes were magnified. His teeth appeared to be made of broken pottery. "All kind of rumors."

The bartender said, "Don't break your spoon stirring that pot, Edmund."

Edmund shrugged and disappeared.

"I know the stories," Beck said, feeling he was being called on to justify himself, his worth. To some oddball prying into their business? The beer elevated his voice to make sure Edmund heard. Make sure the whole town heard: We belong here. "That land's been in my family for a hundred years. Built by my great-grandparents."

"There's been accidents," the bartender said, "but they're just accidents. People scare easy."

From the booth Edmund expelled a stream of smoke.

Beck drained his beer. Nodded when the bartender asked about another round.

"The freezer stuff," Mallory said. "Don't want it to thaw."

Beck didn't answer.

When drinks arrived Mallory said she didn't want it. Beck drank half of hers in a gulp.

"Spooky," he said, all filters melting nicely away. "Spooooky."

"The girls," Mallory said. Her voice was less than a whisper.

"Back to our wrong land," he said in a nasty tone. The water birds at the bar raised their heads.

Mallory went to pay the tab. Beck stared at the back of the smoky booth. "Edmund. The crime-solving dog."

Mallory returned. "Let's go."

Beck appraised his wife, who reddened under his glare. Her lame padded acceptance of everything handed her way. What the fuck was that? No way to live. Hell if his daughters would be like her. He drained her vodka.

"See you, Edmund," he hollered as Mallory dragged him into the blinding light of day.

Tina Randall here, special crow and prosecutor. Here to put the Randalls on trial. Requesting a life sentence or a death penalty and the question is…drum roll… what the heck is the difference?

Threads of dead touch my head. Or maybe those are gnats. I'm sitting under a shady tree, and the tree is also under me. Roots are veins; dirt is skin.

Words are vapor sifting through me. Talk, Bernie. Talk, Lucille. Talk, all of you.

I want to know why I wake up at night. Why I hear the whistle. What it means. What it's telling me to do.

I want to know why I don't remember our first house.

When I looked for photo albums yesterday I couldn't find any. I don't remember my friends. There was a girl who used to sleep over a lot in fifth grade. What was her name? What does she even look like? I don't remember my school, my classroom, my teachers. When I asked Dad where I was born he walked away.

It's not terrible forgetting other people, but I don't want to be forgotten. The forgotten can't forget because they have nothing to remember.

That's why I want to remember you, Bernie Lucille Betty Loren. So you can put us on trial and tell me what we deserve.

Bernie, rudderless boat. They watched him drift from school, from human engagement. Watched him become machine: axe-wielding, gun-firing, game-dressing. His mastery was deer, squirrel, rabbit, wild turkey. They raised hens for eggs, some for food, and he lopped heads and plucked feathers without being asked. Sometimes he impaled the heads on sticks and waved them in Lucille's face or wedged them in the crooks of branches, where they sentried the forest perimeter until ants ate their eyes.

They watched Bernie chew like a cow, neither tasting nor remarking upon his mother's meals. They saw his body grow and mind shrink. He relocated his bed to the pole barn and slept there, saying alone, alone.

At rare times he flashed the original Bernie, fleeting exchanges seized and savored by Lucille, all the more heartbreaking for their brevity.

"You like magic?" he said one afternoon, approaching Lucille as she hung clothes on the line behind the cabin. His squinched eyes seemed half-blind in the sun.

"Of course," she said. She read his face, saw a wisp

of childish mischief there that raised a gust of emotion. "You don't know magic."

"Watch and see." His lips curled, nearly a smile but tentative as if he'd forgotten how.

He dug into a pocket of his overalls and came out with a wooden match gripped in his fist. With a dramatic opening of his hand, the match was gone. Lucille stared in amazement. He watched her expression with a look of satisfaction. He closed his fist again and the match reappeared.

"Impressive," she said. "This what you do in the pole barn all day?"

"Nothing to it," he said, giving her the match. "Just how you looking at things. I'm controlling your perception." He articulated the last word as if he had practiced it as many times as the trick itself. He tapped the side of his head and walked away, back to his cave.

Sometimes Lucille asked about the rabbit: where it was and what he'd done with it. Got shrugs or nothing. She assumed he had killed it; she hadn't heard the whistler since Bernie's three-day vanish. Saw no wooden box nor its remnants.

Lucille kept to her studies. Completed eighth grade, top of the class. Heard about a place that trained nurses downstate near Detroit. When she daydreamed she saw herself clothed in white, leaning over beds to make men strong again. Sometimes she envisioned Bernie in that bed; sometimes her father, who all those years hid his sickness inside. But Pa's sickness was helplessness and maybe the only cure was death. She wondered about good death, if life was at times the crueler outcome. Thought about the forest eater, about purpose and design. Wondered if God intended the forest as garden or grave.

But she didn't believe in God. She had to remind herself of this daily because if not God then what force could raise birdsong breeze branches bees, swirling chaotic symmetry, the sightless breath of wind? It stabbed her deeply to ponder this orchestra as a random die roll. The evolution talk she had heard whispers of set no more easily with her than talk of a creator on a pearly throne. She wondered if answers might in some way be questions.

Lucille entered her bedroom one afternoon and found Bernie naked on her mattress, his flesh like a curved branch in his hand. He stared at her without stopping and bared his teeth. She backed out of the room, heart vibrating, and did not tell her mother what she'd seen. Not many days later she bled as a woman for the first time.

∽

Break-time Camels tasted best. Beck had smoked off and on mostly because his parents hated it. He had never truly enjoyed the ritual until now. Sweaty neck, stained shirt, hands marked with callouses and oil burns—labor brought out the flavor. Who knew? He had worked hard for his engineering degree, served long days at the company, but had never felt so good and used as this. He stood alone behind the restaurant under the yellow light and sipped from his flask.

Shelley stepped outside. He slid the flask into his pocket. After a moment of uneasy glances, she told Beck about her son. She didn't know if it was their business but her boy Noah had been messaging with his girl Lucy. They'd even met each other once.

"I guess you have the right to know," she said.

Anger roiled him. "I don't understand how."

She blew a stream of smoke at the stars. "He snuck over to your place one night." She looked at her feet. "I feel like crap. If my mom had ever read my texts, I would have killed her. Not that we had texts back then, right?"

"Our cabin isn't even on the map." He chuckled affably as if impressed by Noah's resourcefulness, but inside he was sick. Lucy, goddammit. Lying without even trying to ask for permission. Hanging out with boys and doing…what? (What the fuck *would* they be doing, genius?) She can't be doing *that*, can she? A conversation blazed in his head. He remembered drunk girls in the backseat of his dad's Audi. Sloppy tongue kisses, sweaty undertits, ugly endings to awkward thrusts. He spat on the ground. *Noah*, was that really his name?

"I appreciate you telling me," he said. He ground his cigarette under the toe of his shoe. "It's no big deal. I shouldn't be surprised."

"Locked up like a princess in a tower. Guess my boy's knight instinct is kicking in." Shelley smiled uneasily. She seemed embarrassed but also unnerved. Beck sensed his revulsion radiating; he savored her discomfort.

He wanted to keep it that way so he went inside.

❦

Dear Lucille,

I heard the whistler the other night. It woke me from my dream: My family was on their backs on the kitchen floor, all three lined in a row. Their skin was cracked and pale and they were dead but their noses were whistling. I could see the music notes slipping out of their nostrils and hanging in the air and fluttering like little flags.

When I woke up Lucy wasn't in her bed. It was after midnight.

I put a jacket over my pajamas. I could hear the whistler in the woods. The sound was far away but also right next to my ear.

I followed the whistle thinking it was you, Lucille. I wanted it to be you. I want it, present tense. One of your photos kept popping into my head, the one I keep under my pillow. You're squatting by a pile of logs. You're white as a candle and your eyes are empty.

I kept thinking I would see you in the woods. That would have been so nice. We could stay outside like this forever. My Lucille never played with me, not even when we were little. I always thought I was born into the wrong family. She's not my friend like you could be. We would peek in the cabin windows at night and make sure their world is warm.

I found Lucy in a car parked on our road. So dark I couldn't see their faces. Smoke was oozing out the windows like a dragon's mouth. The man was a shadow. I didn't think he was real. Then Lucy kissed him for a long time. I felt scared for her. I heard rustling. On the path was a black rabbit. The one from my dreams. I reached out to pet it and remembered I was still dreaming. *Every day we dream, every night we die.* The rabbit bolted when the headlights came on.

I ran home and climbed into bed and pretended I was asleep.

Why did you kill Bernie? Dad says it was an accident, but he doesn't let me see his eyes anymore. His answer without an answer.

Nights now I sneak outside and search for the rabbit and listen to voices. Will the rabbit help Lucy when she's in trouble? Or will I help? Am I the rabbit?

I'm not going to let my teacher read this one.

❧

Four seasons cycling, thousands of days. Churn of death, life, rebirth.

Forgotten nursing school pamphlets hide in Lucille's bureau. Her life is a phonograph. She wishes she could bump the gramophone, hop the needle, bounce around, and settle wherever but here.

Betty likes her children close. Needs them, truthfully—in particular Lucille. She admits it's selfish to ask her daughter to miss high school, miss young womanhood but cannot think of another way.

Bernie is no brother. Cheeks laced with stubble like moss. Oily hair shaggy. Thick like a man yet malnourished. Spends half of each month not home. Packs a satchel with scant food. Brings shotgun, ammo, no change of clothes. Secretly Lucille wishes he would run away, take up a job in a far-off town, shoot himself in the foot and get eaten by the forest—no, not that. Not dead.

Each month Bernie returns smudged and stinking, shoulders slung with rabbit, squirrel, pheasant. She's never glad to see him, not this way.

He slides into the pole barn and scarcely emerges. Betty forces him to bathe and trims his hair. His eyes float like clouds. In his sleep he still converses with the unseen; his voice carrying from workshop all the way to the cabin. Sometimes he paces the yard, a spirit hollering at spirits.

Some nights Lucille wakes to see his face outside her bedroom window, peering in.

Brother and sister don't talk much. His head is crowded with voices that are not hers. One morning Lucille finds him chopping wood. His shirt is off and his torso is a red roadmap of scratches.

"We have enough wood," she says. Half of her believes he no longer speaks English. Like talking to a tree. It startles her to hear him answer.

"I'm not made to do much else." Sweat pours down his face like his head sprung a leak. He finds Lucille with his eyes. She leans in and sees a whisper in his stare, non-words, a whisper she strains to hear. *Hear.* Hear what?

"Why do you leave?" she asks. "You could hunt from home, Bernie."

His name in her mouth tastes of violation, like swallowing liver when expecting chocolate.

A light flickers in him, an innocence gathering in his eyes, the unspoiled boy she once knew. "I'm protecting you," he says.

At eighteen, Lucille has taken a job at the restaurant in town. Cleans and waits tables, handles the register, prepares food when the cook is home sick. She walks the same path each day and is grateful for the illusion of movement.

The money helps, and Lucille buys groceries at the Wolfolk store. She picks up mail at the postal office; although the box is usually empty, she checks it whenever she can. She stops at the library to read newspapers from Chicago, Detroit, Cleveland. She loves looking at the clothing, reading about theater, music, dance, pictures that move.

For months she hears about the Great European War. Some wonder why the United States wants to get involved. Others say it's overdue. Word among town folk is that our boys will have to register for a draft. Everyone over twenty-one.

The WHS Fall Social was set for Friday, October 20th. Seven p.m. Beck learned details from Shelley.

Beck worked Friday and Saturday nights. Weekends were all-hands-on-deck.

Lucy would only need to sneak out without her mother noticing. Not difficult. Mallory was no natural-born observer. She took people at face value. Never suspicious. A person needed a healthy suspicion to succeed in life: the one useful thing Beck's father had taught him.

Lucy would claim to be ill. Pretend to be asleep. Get Tina to lie for her. Simple.

But Lucy was in for a surprise.

Beck didn't blame her. He understood her motivation. It wasn't long ago that he was sneaking out, meeting girls—at the riverside, at the graveyard, in the parking lot behind the bowling alley. Dishonesty was once necessity, and Beck wore deception like skin.

Painful to admit it but he knew he'd inherited this gift from his father. His father always had two or three women on the side. Poor Mom waited, blind or complacent, probably blind, willfully or not. Men were pigs, plain and simple. Beck did not exempt himself from this adage. A man would destroy family, career, self-respect. Dangle a girl in front of him, and he abandoned reason, decency, control. His own father's foolish lapdog expression every time a leggy woman stood near was pathetic. Wag that tongue, Dad. Atta boy, Dad. Yeah, sure, nobody notices.

After high school, Beck resolved to chain his desires. Met Mallory his first year of college and committed to her. Burned his yearbooks in a backyard pyre. Those books represented playboy Beck, the entitled asshole who screwed half his class and was known as *boy slut*. Friendships ruined by jealousy. Drunken fistfights. The abortion she wasn't keen on getting. Ugly, ugly. Alone, he moved to the university and never looked back.

Cold night of dancing trees. Branches rake the cabin walls.

She was sleeping-then-not. Sleeping-then-not. Restless with a pit inside. Wind moaning like an anguished woman. No moon. Her bedroom was lightless as a cave.

Hours or moments later she woke again. The whistler: she had heard it. Was it a dream? It had been so many years. She waited, eyes closed and dancing along the edge of unconscious. Then it whistled again through the howling gusts, a melody precarious and distant as a child's knock. The tune was the same as years ago, but now the whistler spoke to Lucille only. Urging. Or mourning. Or warning. Or all?

She opened her eyes. In the corner of the room stood a shadow. A man. He climbed on top of her. The hand muffling her mouth stank of soil and sweat. She bucked and heaved but he was solid and held her fast. She breathed his shaving soap and wanted to scream but was afraid. His breath was fire on her face as he ripped her nightgown. His fingers pushed into her mouth and gagged her. She bit down and tasted blood. He grunted, scorching her below.

In the morning she washed and gathered eggs and moved without seeing and instead of walking to work headed deep into the woods with the shotgun. For six hours she stared at nothing, felt nothing while bugs graced her skin. Was she a tree. Was she a person. Was she here at all. The pain between her legs the loudest answer.

She needed the rabbit to appear. The black rabbit, her father's soul. She believed this. He had tried to warn her by whistling through the wind. She needed him again. Tears dampened her face. She needed permission for what she intended, the shotgun cradled on her lap. She intended to feed herself both barrels against this jack pine, but when she saw the fawn and mother stepping gingerly between trees twenty yards distant she aimed and blew apart the baby's head and went home.

∂๑

Lucy offered Tina twenty bucks to shut her face and help her escape.

"I know you followed me," Lucy said.

Tina kept typing. The sisters were on the swing but not swinging.

"I'm talking to you." Lucy punched Tina's shoulder.

"I'll take your money." Tina's smile was a child's sandcastle, misshapen and confusing and ready to melt at first wave.

"If I give you the money, it means you'll help."

"Why do you like that guy?" Tina slid the folded bill into her jeans pocket.

"None of your business."

"I think he's ugly."

"Now you're pissing me off."

Tina stopped typing. "Not ugly on the outside. Here, here, here." She pointed to Lucy's head, heart, groin.

Lucy stood up and kicked the swing. "You're a fucking baby."

Tina pulled the twenty from her pocket and held it forth like a filthy rag.

"Just keep it." Lucy sat back down. "Tomorrow night at dinner. Dad will be at work. You have to beg Mom to take you fishing. Don't take no for an answer.

Noah's picking me up at seven, so I need to leave by 6:45."

Tina set aside her laptop, took Lucy's hands, slipped the money into Lucy's palm.

"What are you doing?"

"I'll help you," Tina said, staring with intensity, "because you're my *sister.*"

When he came again she was ready. She had snuck the butcher's knife into bed and as he mounted her pressed its edge against his throat.

Blind, entranced, uncaring, he continued his mission. She fought tears. She wanted to cut him but couldn't. Shameful heat burned clean up to her throat, a fire of pain but worse, disgust, hatred. Unable to let the knife speak, she lay soundless until he finished.

During the day Bernie acted no different. No acknowledgment that he'd done wrong. Mother seemed to suspect nothing, but over supper her gaze lingered on Lucille. Maybe she sensed detachment, sensed the throttling of her daughter's spirit but did not ask the reason. Supper was a song of flatware clinking. Lucille prayed that he would get called to the War: *please take him so he's lost forever.*

Five weeks after Bernie's second visit, Lucille missed

her monthly blood. Soon after, she vomited on her morning walk and lay in the shade until the nausea passed. She arrived at the restaurant late and sullen and sick.

The third visit was Lucille going to Bernie's room.

Nighttime brought no sleep, but the whistler came louder than ever. The melody filled her with courage. She climbed from the bed, lit the lantern, and went outside. Her breath billowed in the chill. Under starless sky she met the rabbit between cabin and pole barn. It stood upright on its haunches with nose atwitch. Lucille's tears leapt like rain. "Smile for me," she said, and when it did she recognized him. When he told her what to do, she listened.

Bernie's door creaked, hinges craving oil. His room was cramped, a ten-by-ten workspace adjoining the barn proper. At the scream of hinges Bernie did not rouse under his mound of blankets. The air stunk of piss and moldy bread. He took most meals in this windowless cave and disallowed even their mother from intruding. Lantern held aloft, Lucille searched walls, shelves, floor, unsure what she was seeking. Tools hung from nails like decorations. Her fingers brushed each implement: claw hammer, crescent wrench, saw, axe, hatchet, hand drill, hoe, shovel. At last she found a coil of rope.

In her mind she pictured Bernie in the clearing at the bloody tree stump. One fierce blow from his axe. Another. He tossed the bodies. The birds ran and flapped, frantic, already dead but unable to know it.

Heads wedged into the crooks of trees.

She tied one end of the rope to the bed frame, ran the line beneath the bed, drew it over Bernie, ran it beneath the bed again and then back across. She repeated this five times, leaving slack to slide the blankets from him. He lay naked but did not wake. His member hid like a grub in a pile of moss. She didn't care whether he woke. She cinched the rope and knotted the end.

Bernie's eyes opened. She didn't recognize him.

Ghostly and weak in his daze, he reminded her of Father at his death. But, no, her father was not a woodworm. Father was a branch, a bloom. This creature was blight.

When he tried to move and met the restraints, he laughed as if it was a game between them. His mirthful laugh drenched her. She couldn't breathe but didn't feel the need, felt power like something bloodless.

She laid the teeth on his Adam's apple. His laugh became gurgles as she sawed. Waves erupted from him, washing them both. He writhed against the squeaking ropes. The rush of his bowels soured the air. Blade hit bone and yet he was alive, aware. His mouth grinned like a child who'd eaten too much cherry pie.

Soon his face wobbled, limp and un-muscled; the blunt snap of the spine. She yanked his oily hair. Even with head detached his eyes would not let go, and she knew how stupid she had been. Headless, he would visit her. Headless, he would not remember her name. How absurd to believe this flimsy metal band capable of halting the devil.

Lucille heard the scream before she knew it was her own.

She screamed as she couldn't while he was on top of her, killing her. As she couldn't every night since, alone and numb upon the shameful mattress. As she couldn't when she spat at her face in the mirror. She loosed a shredded cry that brought Mother from sleep to pole barn.

Tore Mother into the shared unclean nightmare.

Dear Lucille,

I know why you did it. I'm wrecked about it. My grandfather was your shame but not your secret. You didn't get rid of him even though your mom wanted you to. You told your mom you were pregnant and you ran away and that's why we're all here now. Here in life, here at the cabin, here on this land in this air. The trees are your smile now.

You wonder how I know. It wasn't hard to listen. The melody said it. The dreams. The pictures. The breeze and the voices. The whistler is you, right? All of you. The rabbit isn't boy or girl. It's a she and a he and a you and a me.

She's the upturned dirt sculpted into fur. He is caution and hope. She lifts me out of sleep, into sleep, little nighttime steps through the dark of the now-past. He doesn't use words. I saw her by the pole barn in the night. He was waiting for me. Her head changed into Bernie's head, Bernie's face. I saw Bernie's head on the bunny! She hopped around the weeds looking afraid with tears wetting his cheeks. I could tell she was my great-grandpa, the one never-named until now. And also she was you at the same time.

Every night I study my dad's fingerprints on the whiskey bottle. They form a frown and a boomerang and a pair of horns. Sadness, return, protection.

Now I understand why my father never calls home or speaks of his parents.

But I wanted to know for sure. I called my grandpa last week and asked: *Who is your father? What's his name?*

He breathed into the phone. I never knew breath

could speak like that. Then he told me I'm a good girl and that he loves me.

At night my father stares at the TV. He smells like burgers and drink. I settle up against him on the couch and feel his heat. It makes me sleepy like a drug. He pushes me away after not-too-long because he's got the sickness. His answer without answer.

Nights he sat on the porch swing, facing the dark. He felt vibrations here beyond civilization where wind was primal breath. A pulse like electricity hummed inside the living land, urges and impulses disconnected from moral law. A breath, a pulse, an urge, but were they contagious? Was this the inevitable fate of animal man?

Being out here was a mistake, he knew now, but a mistake Beck needed. A calculated error to press him into his prescribed shape like those holiday cookie cutters his mother used to use. Face his fate and his past and say fuck it. He had to walk with ghosts if he was ever going to not become one.

Why was his father so determined not to sell him this land? What was he afraid Beck would learn? Why would his parents never visit?

Beck's anger at Lucy grew, but now he welcomed the feeling into his blood. Anger could be concern could be love. The only emotion his own father invested in him was annoyance, Beck the circling fly.

He trusted Lucy the way his father never trusted him. His father kept tabs, kept score, distrusted for control rather than love.

Beck had drank and drugged and slept around and did petty vandalism, stupid stuff. His goal was to give the old man a reason for his paranoia, to say, "Hey, Dad, I'm everything you feared. I'm you." He tried to gut the old man with his own rectitude. He did not want to be his father. But it twisted him to think about Noah acting toward his daughter the way he, Beck, had acted toward young women.

A few nights before the dance Beck stepped into the girls' room to say good night. Lucy, in a blue T-shirt with blue panties underneath, set her phone on the stand and climbed under the covers. Straight brown hair, long brown legs. Her body had rounded in every womanly place.

"I know about your secret," he said, "with that boy." He heard his tone of authority and disapproval and felt a flutter of something like pride, maybe righteousness. He hadn't said what he meant but had meant what he said. "I work with Noah's mother." He took pleasure in watching her face deflate, her lip tremble. "Don't say anything. I'm hurt but not mad."

Tears formed in her eyes, but he knew Lucy. Not a crier unless she was angry. So she was angry. Probably at Noah's mother. Probably not at him. Beck could save face, could look like the hero.

"I haven't told your mom yet, but I want you to know I'm okay with it." He produced a casual laugh and said, "I'd love to meet this young man."

Tina jolted upright in bed like a yanked puppet. "You're letting her go? You don't even know him."

"It's nice of you to care," Lucy said.

"You shut up."

"Girls, please."

"She doesn't even *know* him."

"God, you're so two-faced." Lucy threw a barrette, missed.

Beck didn't know what was happening. Something complicated between sisters he did not want to untwine. He had never understood women, and now his daughters were them.

"He's a bad man," Tina said.

"Shut up, idiot."

"Stop," Beck said. "Both of you."

"Don't listen to her," Lucy said.

"I'm sure you mean well, but, Tina, you aren't in this conversation."

"I'm not in this world," Tina said. She buried her

head under a pillow and hummed a short, distinctive melody.

"Fucking twerp," Lucy said.

"Girls. Enough." He felt hollow and ineffectual, craving a drink. What could he do, ground them? Their life here was an eternal grounding. "We aren't talking any more about it. Get some sleep."

"You can't meet him," Lucy said.

Beck paused in the doorway.

"You're working that night."

He nodded and flipped the switch.

❧

Did you bear the blame?

Did your ma say it was your fault?

Does every man have the sickness?

❧

Betty found Lucille on the floor of the workshop. The airborne profanities sickened her nose and throat. The room was painted like a slaughterhouse.

Lucille cradled the head, brushing fingers through the knotty hair. The skin papery, eyes stones.

On the bed the corpse reposed, a waxen thing in a crimson pool, a storefront mannequin Betty had seen as a child on a trip to Flint. Wan and inhuman, not her flesh.

They rolled body into blanket then dragged blanket and mattress to the yard. Betty fetched kerosene and doused everything but the head. The flames swelled and breathed, black smoke vining into the sky.

Lucille wanted to ascend the column like Jack's beanstalk but felt the feeble despair of the earthbound.

Lucille lost her insides on the grass, the taste in her mouth sweet like sap.

Not once did Betty ask why she'd done it. Her answer without answer.

Ashen and blood-soaked they watched the pyre. Lucille craved her mother's absolution. Not speaking felt like a form of condemnation.

Betty wouldn't burn the head, demanding a burial. She made Lucille use the cloth bag for gathering vegetables.

❧

Why did you kill?
Because you had hands.
Why did you run?
Because you had legs.

I have hands. I have legs.

❧

Betty turned hard and lean in mind and shape.

Whenever in the woods, Lucille steered wide of Bernie's mound, eyeballing it as if daring him to crawl out of there. She saw crows light upon and peck the earth. She watched rain fall everywhere but his grave. One morning a half-dozen shrews had pilgrimaged to die on that spot. Nights when Lucille couldn't sleep, her belly grown taut, she peered out the window and saw the whistler on the mound, baring its human teeth.

Lucille imagined birthing a baby made of rock. The baby would be invulnerable, a flame-handler, a mocker of light and laughter, an earth-tempered mineral no hand could break.

Her mother ate thin broth and homegrown vegetables but not much else.

❧

Friday, October 20th. Beck wakes in the night. Two a.m. His head is pounding, mouth dry. Mallory, a blanketed lump beside him, whistles through her nose. Chilly tiles under his feet, Beck steps into the kitchen for a glass of water. He had worked second shift on Thursday, a few hours ago, came home at ten p.m. The family—Tina, Lucy, Mallory—was in a happy mood. At the dining table they greeted him with smiles, and was this the new normal? Was allowing his daughter to go to a dance the key? Biting the tongue, tamping down fear, living in denial: the keys to joy.

They played a game together, the family. Mallory popped corn on the stove. Beck put Dizzy on the stereo. As they rattled a canister of dice, filled in their scores, yelled *Kismet!*, Tina called him Daddy and refilled his glass and rested her hand on his arm and told him he was strong and that it made her hungry to sit by him because he smelled like french fries. Lucy was talkative, open, like she used to be. (Did she used to be like that? He couldn't recall.) Nobody mentioned the dance or the boy Noah. The whole evening…was it a dream? Tina's smile, come to think of it, seemed incorrect. Crooked and thin like a mask. As if he could reach out and peel it away. Was it only a dream? No, certainly not. He made love to Mallory after the girls went to bed. Only hours ago but it feels like years.

It's two a.m. It's still two a.m. How long has he been standing here in the kitchen holding an empty glass? The window over the sink frames unbroken blackness. Beck's faded reflection hovers there, soft as a memory. On the counter he locates the bottle and takes a few slugs. There's a torn shred of paper taped to the bottom of the bottle.

YOUR FATHER BROUGHT YOU HERE ASK HIM WHY.

Primitive block letters, pencil, resembling Beck's own handwriting.

YOUR FATHER BROUGHT YOU HERE ASK HIM WHY.

Everyone asleep. Ticking wall clock reads two a.m. His father's idea. His father convinced him to buy this land, convinced Beck to move his family there. Didn't he? No. Or yes. The memories are quiet puffs of air, invisible. Beck can't recall when the deed was signed, or why. He drinks more whiskey and locates Mallory's phone. His father's number is programmed, a good thing because Beck can't remember it.

Did Beck write that note? He dons a flannel and steps outside to ask the wind. Cold invasive hands he cannot see grope him through his shirt. On the porch swing he stares blankly at the fuzzy shape of the pole barn. Trees form in gradations of gray as his eyes adjust.

On the first ring an answer: his father, shouting and awake and breathless. "Mallory my dear how nice of you to call how's the family!"

"You got what you wanted," Beck says.

"Who is this state your business I'm a busy man getting my five miles in spit it out I don't have all day."

Beck stands, shaking with anger. The wooden swing bumps his calves. "You know who this is, and you know what you did. Tell me why."

"There's a line drawn down the center of you."

"Tell me why you sent us here."

"Is this the last time you called or will there be more I expected to hear from you but not until you were dead."

Dad, please. Please tell me.

"You're a coin."

Please.

"You on the grill yes you you're burned on one side ready to be flipped what time is it there and why do you sound like a woman."

Please.

Beck's breath expels and swirls, a frozen moment here and gone. His father's voice is fading as if the phone has shrunk and is now a wood chip.

There is movement in the yard. Against the pole barn leans a shadow. Moonlight flickers behind clouds. Beck steps barefoot onto the chilly hard ground. Against the pole barn leans a shadow, a boy in denim overalls. Wool fishing cap on his head. A knotty boy with a wide face and eclipsed eyes made of shadow against the pole barn. It takes so much time to reach him. So many steps with breath coming fast as the barn and the boy leaning against it retreat, retreat.

Panting, Beck arrives. Or near enough. "Are you Noah? You can't be here."

The boy, silent, rearranges his face into flesh. A frown wriggles onto his mouth. He pushes open the side door which groans or he groans who can tell. Beck follows the boy into the workshop. Air made of oil and sawdust. No light but the moon paints shapes of saw-horses and mowers. Tools glint on the wall.

The boy faces away. Back to Beck he speaks in the high voice of a young girl: "I used to sleep in this room. Will you touch me? You smell delicious."

"You can't be here." Beck grips the boy's shoulders, turns him sharply. Shakes him. He is soft not boneless. The cap falls first, and then the head falls thud thump.

Beck kneels with brick in hand. Again and again, the brick falls, fucking the face open. Gliding arcs of blood grace air as squealing bones rupture. An eyeball slides free from the socket.

Afterward Beck nestles the boy and awakens with a pillow in his arms.

❧

"Your father is sick."

"Our father will not get well."

"Our father is sick."

"Your father sleeps behind a paper mask."

"Drawn with a line down his center."

"Your father needs sleep."

"Our father is son and daughter and his nose whistles."

❧

Lucy couldn't. Wouldn't. Homework could wait.

She'd been messaging Noah all morning with no reply.

"Your father is sick."

Mom stepped onto the porch with drinks.

"I'm sick too," Tina moaned. She held her stomach. Abdomen, really.

Mom, sighing, touched Tina's head. Lucy understood. Three years ago her mother had touched her the same way.

"You don't have to finish your homework."

"What about me?" Lucy said.

"Let's all take a sick day."

"What's wrong with Daddy?" Tina said.

Daddy. No wonder, Lucy thought. Gets her first period and regresses to age four.

"Your father needs sleep."

A buzz. A notification. Noah finally.

So I can actually come up to the house?? Do I have to meet them lol

❧

How long was sleep? The bedside clock read two in red.

Not how long but how deep. That is the correct question.

Still two a.m.? A narcotic drowsiness squeezed, fluttered his lids.

He forced his eyes open. Sunlight haloed the curtain. Lips: painfully dry. He felt nauseous and belched and saw he was spooning a headless body: The boy in denim overalls with a great empty hole where a head once lived.

The face, the brick, the savage blows.

No, a pillow. A pillow in his arms. An erection straining his pajamas. God, he was ill.

Not a boy's face, his father's: skintorn mass, bonebusted, eyeball dangling.

He sat up breathless and filmy with sweat. Palm and fingers tender and puffy.

Mallory stood bedside with a washcloth. Stay down, she said. You're on fire.

Beck shoved her aside, lumbered through kitchen and entryway, staggered unseeing against the brightness, dimly conscious of wife and daughters imploring, their voices distant and melodious like the whistle he now hears, a simple melody like fingers descending his icy feverish body. He stumbles across the lawn to the pole barn, rams his shoulder against the workshop door, unsticks it—the damn door always stuck, the damn sloppy paint job.

There on the concrete floor between mower, table saw, and woodchipper are droplets of blood.

Just a few drops. Baby tears. He touches them. Damp.

He swoons, feels his body falling.

✧

Does he know what happened to his body?

Does he walk the woods looking for his mother's bones?

Do the wasps drone, the bees hum, the flies buzz in the voices of the slain?

✧

Dear Lucille:

Last night I learned bleeding. The whistler let me in or I let the whistler in. I can't tell the difference. There is none no nope.

I was crunching through the forest, shivering in my pajamas, sticks jabbing my feet. Over the tree frog buzz and loon laugh I heard the whistle but couldn't find it.

The next minute I was in the workshop with someone. Great-Grandpa Loren or my dad or Grandpa. A man with plenty of faces anyway and I was safe and hugging the whistler to my chest. The whistler's hair was warm and soft.

I wanted the man to touch me. I told him so. Why shouldn't the man with faces touch me? I closed my eyes to make the world blacker so he could touch me.

I wanted him to touch me but not that way.

He pinched my shoulders and shook me. My thighs got wet. My head fell off.

Her mother actually helped.

She'd never seen her mother so pleased. They spread out makeup on the table, the bathroom too cramped. Mom brought out the hand mirror for the occasion. Lucy's first big dance. Mom wasn't mad that she'd lied; she wanted to hear about this Noah.

How could Lucy explain that she liked him okay, he was fine but was a means to an end? She knew this wasn't what Mom wanted to hear so she spun gold from thread, played coy while hinting that he was special. Speaking to her mother unguardedly hadn't happened in years. Days earlier the idea would have been inconceivable. Now her mother swabbed Lucy's eyelashes, sitting so close Lucy could see the penny-sized birthmark under her left collarbone, could smell the almond butter on her breath, could read the age lines on her throat. So many hours, Lucy realized, had been wasted hating this woman. Now Lucy saw that her mother was only skin over bones over organs, a delicate machine bearing no malice and carrying not maternal love but a semblance, certainly maternal caring, certainly desiring good for Lucy and Tina. This was not a person to run from or to battle but a person to keep close and tell simple lies to because that was all she required.

Mother styled Lucy's hair while Lucy described her thoughts on the future, her plans and hopes. She had never opened up like this; not to anyone. Her mother's gentle tugging at her scalp produced a funny feeling in her stomach and she knew without knowing why that this would be the last time she would be so close to this woman.

Am I supposed to see Bernie or be Bernie. The difference is none none none.

He was visited. Family stood in dreams unsmiling at the foot of his bed: Loren, Betty, Bernie, Lucille. He hadn't recognized the boy in the workshop but now of course, of course. Now he understood what his father could never say. Now he saw the old man as doomed and broken and trapped. Beck was overwhelmed by helpless love. He sucked the air, trying to swallow it all but never getting enough. He wept until his lids fell with sleep.

Mallory brought washcloths and water. She attacked the fever, helping him swallow pills. Nothing brought the temperature down. She wanted to take him to a hospital, but Beck said her only job was to protect Lucy. He said *protect* or thought he had said it; Mallory, however, only smiled and patted his leg. She hadn't heard or didn't care? He shouted that Lucy was in danger, tried to move but the covers weighed hundreds of pounds and when he opened his eyes he lay alone in the milky dying daylight.

❧

Beautiful Lucy stood.

Beautiful Lucille stood.

Tina watched them twirl as one person before the long mirror.

"Noah had so much faith," Tina said. "He didn't even mind that God destroyed the world."

"How about for one night you leave me alone."

"Noah and his family were all that mattered. The rest could go to hell."

"Starting your own Sunday school?"

"What would you do if you woke up and were somebody else?"

"I might give a shit for once."

"So it would be a good thing."

Lucy faced Tina with cold eyes. "I need you to go away."

"You look so much like her."

Lucy didn't answer. Finished her grooming and turned to leave.

"Lucille," Tina said. She had to bring it up while she still had the chance. Before everything happened. "You might even *be* her."

The knock came, four stiff raps. One for each member of our family, Tina thought.

"If I'm her," Lucy said, "who does that make you?"

The rain began, a steady lashing on the roof.

Betty sat at the dining table with a mug of coffee between her hands. It was her sixtieth birthday. She was alone. Her radio played a George Gershwin song that reminded her of her pa; he'd been dead for a decade. When the notice had come Betty regarded it as one would a photograph of an exotic place she'd visited in youth: detached curiosity and wistfulness. His name on the paper looked like an arrangement of twigs. The dead had settled in around her for years, gotten comfortable with the furniture. She had no cause to grieve her father's passing. He would find a foothold where love could accommodate him; it wasn't this place.

The bedroom where Lucille used to sleep, and before that Lucille and Bernie slept, exhaled. Twice a day it breathed or groaned. Betty would fill it with bricks if she could.

Instead, the whisper of children's feet and small boy sobs from under the earth ushered her into dreams each evening.

❦

What we see:

A vehicle slowing along County Road 93 and turning onto the dirt drive. The sky is the white of fish scales; dusk. Even before entering the dark mouth of the woods its headlights are on, two bright eyes without feeling, exposing both the healthy and broken as it casts among the trees.

A carriage in the shape of nothing here, molded by fire and noise. A body red as a cardinal. A Jeep Cherokee nosing like a hound along the one-lane. In spite of the uneven path, the ride is relatively steady and smooth.

Behind the wheel is a young man in a baby blue formal jacket and white bow tie. On the passenger seat rests a clear plastic box containing a white calla lily.

What we see:

A car the shape of a box, molded by fire and noise. A Jeffery Six Touring manufactured in Kenosha, Wisconsin. A car with no roof. A car with white tires and a body black as a crow. A car that sways wildly along the lumpy lane.

Behind the wheel is a young man wearing an olive green sacksuit and brown necktie. A hat on his head. On the seat beside him is a folder of papers. He is beginning to feel queasy.

The threads are thicker than she thought. A coil of rope unearthed from a pile of scrap wood, heavy and coarse and hairy. She breathes air of the past, this rope the same one that bound Bernie: could it be? If not the same then certainly cousin, daughter, Great-Grandrope.

She has heard trees in a stiff breeze, ancient trunks whining as if infants are trapped within. All the players of this forest narrating regret, growth, pain, joy. Beyond sight is a vastness that wants to live inside us. The whistler is the bridge, she thinks, between humankind and our wooden selves.

Tina knows what to do—for them, for himherituswcthem. Now she knows that her obituary was not written for her but for Lucy, poor Lucy whose name was never her own. Maybe not a literal death but an undertaking. She will do this for her sister. Take the kernel into herself and give back this heart to the forest.

She removes pants, shirt, socks, underwear. A pile of shucked skin. The makeup binds strangely to her face, cakey and dry, but in the dimness she senses Lucille and Bernie and Betty and Loren and the hurt. Their words never fell silent, endless speaking in whisper gusts. Pain the seed. Rape the victory. Shame the salvation.

Bernie's sin was ghastly but created their lives, all of them. Without him there would be no Tina, Lucy, Daddy. She would be blackness unvoiced. Sin as necessity; sin as savior. Like Judas's betrayal.

She hears the engine approaching. Wraps the cord around herself like a bandage, legs to waist to belly to heart. She lays naked on the cold cement how Bernie laid. She tries to whistle, wets her lips. Tries again. The song is born.

☙

A faraway hum like a horsefly but deeper, mechanical. Rattling like her father's chest.

An automobile. Lucille had seen a few in Wolfolk and recognized the sound. Her breath caught as she parted her bedroom curtains and saw the vehicle ease into the clearing.

At six months pregnant she was not too inhibited to lower onto all fours and slide the valise from beneath the bed, the valise purchased with months of saved wages, a nickel at a time. Inside: two changes of clothing, a nursing school brochure, a stack of family photographs.

She heard the stiff creak of the pole barn door. Outside the window stood Ma with spade in hand.

The young man held a Homburg hat to his stomach. Lucille's wink toward the stars, her voiceless wish, was younger than she expected. His mustache looked like a caterpillar. Within his soft cadence Lucille caught phrases: —*federal selective services…Bernard Loren Randall…all men of age twenty-one must register*—and this reminded Lucille to retrieve the government letter from underneath the bedside table. She put it atop her clothes and buttoned up the valise.

"Don't know where he gone," her ma was saying as Lucille emerged from the cabin. "Took off a few weeks ago."

The man nodded at Lucille and noticed the valise. "You live here, miss?"

Lucille's mother also saw the valise; her face became a drinking glass tipped and emptied.

"That's his sister," Betty said. "She ain't seen him."

"That correct, miss?"

The valise felt full of stones. "He's not here any-more." Tears dropped down Lucille's cheeks.

"It's a federal offense to not register with selective services." The young man's brow shined as sunglow gathered close. "I hope you all aren't assisting Bernard in this crime."

Betty turned the spade in her hands.

"Take me with you," Lucille said.

"Excuse me?"

"Please," she said, and as in a dream she stepped toward him. She felt separate from her body as she gripped his shoulder. "Take me away from here."

Betty frowned. "Not like this," she said.

"She's keeping me against my will."

The man attempted to withdraw from Lucille's grasp. "I don't think this is my concern."

"Please," Betty said, "take the unholy bitch. A pound of gamy flesh is what she carries, and I am pink to be rid of her."

Betty raised the shovel like a baseball bat and swung it near enough the man's face that he stumbled back against the wheel cover, breaking a headlight with his wayward elbow. Ashen and stunned he kept an eye on Betty while helping Lucille into the backseat.

"I will free them," Betty said. "That is a promise." Her hair resembled shaggy soldier weed, hysterical eyes unseeing. "The tick is plucked loose. We're gonna dance under the moon, and you are uninvited. Me and my men forever." She flashed sallow teeth, and her scored skin appeared halfway to dust.

The automobile kicked up dirt as the man slammed the pedal down. Lucille in the backseat stared at the sky, the canopy of trees, until closing her eyes. She felt herself being swept along like a leaf on a river, with welcome violence. The man drove too fast. Her body bounced, both weightless and heavy, the ungiving seat battering the breath from her lungs. She dreamed that her baby was forever asleep. Thank you, thank you went her mind.

Mixed among the clatter and smoke were the final words Lucille heard from her mother:

"My neck is stronger than his!"

It sounded like part of the forest; a far hum, a swarm.

A Jeep Cherokee was birthed into the clearing. Dusk had fallen, daylight silently away. Noah parked beside the Randalls' pickup truck. He'd been expecting Lucy to be waiting outside. Not that she said she would; her messages were just so eager that it sounded like she would bound into his arms. But the cabin was hushed, draped windows holding a butter shine. His mother had warned him: Lucy's father was a drinker. Everyone at the restaurant knew it but he did his job well so they let it slide. *Still*, his mother said, *keep an eye open*.

He checked his hair in the rearview, smoothed his eyebrows, spritzed his neck with Axe. His first formal dance. *Send pictures*, his mother had said. Dad had moved out seven years ago and lived up at Mullet Lake. All for the best since the guy was a meth head of the chronic variety.

From somewhere far away came a faint whistling. A melody like a signal. A soft welcome, although from whom he didn't know.

Noah knocked on the door. Waited with corsage tucked under arm. Knocked again a bit harder. He peered into the dim kitchen. A table, appliances. No person.

He typed a quick text to Lucy: *I'm here where r u*

He heard moans from inside the cabin. He slid the phone into his pocket. The door was unlocked so he opened it.

An entryway for shoes. Short hallway heading left. Bathroom on the right. Kitchen ahead. A sour smell hanging like a body unwashed. The moans, louder now, are hard to interpret. Coming from behind the closed door just off the kitchen. A bass-voice moan. Gravelly. Groan of pain? Terror? Animal pleasure? Or perhaps misery, searing and slow, song of death.

Before him stands a closed door. Aware of every creaking step, he approaches. Inside is the man—outside, the boy, nervous and uncertain in his formalwear, corsage in a plastic box gripped tight. The boy presses an ear against the wood, heart giving tremors to his body.

The moaning stops.

He waits. Five seconds. Ten. The longest thirty he has known.

Should he turn the knob? Could Lucy be in there?

But then another noise: a girl yelling for help. Distant and muffled. Inside something, possibly buried in the earth it sounds so faint. Where is it coming from? He steps away from the door, crosses the kitchen, peers into a room with two beds. Lucy and Tina's bedroom, must be.

Help. Help me, Noah.

She is calling his name.

The voice comes from outside but sounds inside. Is it possible to be both at once?

The pole barn, of course. His family has a pole barn too, and he's heard his sister yelling from inside it. His face burns. The voice is loud, desperate.

Outside he bashes the porch swing with his thigh, sends it jerking and flailing, sprints across the clearing and yanks the wrought-iron handle. The plastic box with the corsage glitters on the grass like a jewel.

With a pop the door unseals, casting evening light across a blackened room, a room with a single clouded window, a room of heaped wood and scrap metal and a freezer and a pegboard of tools and the blood of every machine puddled in spots on the concrete, snowblower, lawnmower, hedgeclipper, weedwhipper, tablesaw, implements designed to reshape life, to sculpt a world greater than God could think of, a world to better serve man, shortsighted God bequeathing the earth to us but not equipping us to live in it—only to die in it unless we yoke beasts and scar the land and fell trees and hammer wood into boxes for shelter and imprisonment and free us to hide from prying eyes all of our weakest shames.

A girl lies on the floor, naked and bound by rope.

Take me. Take me. Take me.

Her eyes are bright and black, shadowed ecstasy on her red lips, a mask of adulthood painted and drawn on this child.

Are you Tina?

Of course she is, so she answers yes, although she laughs inside knowing she's been Tina only for a blink in the grand scheme and is also other people other than

Tina, mixed up like different colors of sand, something she saw at a wedding once long ago when bride and groom poured green and blue sand into a bottle and the priest shook it up and intoned, "Just as these grains of sand can now never be separated, so too shall this man and woman remain entwined. What was once two separate people has now formed a new person."

A new person.

Noah is pulling off the ropes. He is more handsome than she wanted to admit to Lucy. His eyes are bullets. He has a rapturous heart.

Take me.

Where? The hospital? Are you hurt?

He sees blood on the floor, a few drops, baby tears.

Take me, Noah.

His face crumples in confusion. This rope isn't even tied.

Take me.

She kisses his lips, wraps her arms around his head, a firm hug so he can't pull away.

He is cologne and saliva and peppermint. He is candy.

Beck has heard the screams too. Muscles flaccid, head throbbing, he is pinned to the mattress (tied?). But it's

Tina and she's calling for help. He'll climb through this rope, this fucking cobweb, this smothering fucking cobweb that somebody laid on top of him even though he is absolutely ON FIRE.

❧

Forty minutes ago:

"Why do I need to do this?"

"Tina wanted to do something special for you. I think it's sweet."

Lucy and Mallory walked along a path through the woods. The sun hung low, twilight October, warmer than expected. The smell of autumn on the wind, the trees rusted ombre in spectacular death.

Tina had told Lucy she prepared a beautiful diorama of nature. Mom could take pre-dance pictures there to send to relatives. She had actually called her "Lucille," and Mother laughed. Whimsy, whimsy.

Noah wasn't arriving until 6:15. They had plenty of time.

As they stepped through high weeds Lucy felt a wedge falling away inside her. She thought about how she, Lucy, had treated Tina her whole life. Excluded her from everything, wanted nothing to do with her. It hadn't felt cruel as Lucy did these things; it felt like the natural order of the world; of course an older sister should shun her younger one. When Lucy was five she had asked her father who he loved more. Beck answered both, the same. Lucy was wounded. The answer made no sense; she loved cats more than dogs; chocolate ice cream over vanilla. Her father must be lying because he loved Tina more. Lucy was only a child herself, couldn't be blamed now, but at the time she stopped thinking of Tina as a sister and saw her as a roadblock.

"Your first big dance," Mallory was saying. "Or at least I think it is. Have you been to a formal dance before?"

"No, Mom."

"Funny that I can't remember. So much of our old life is just…gone. Anyway, you look breathtaking."

"This hike is taking your breath. Where is this place, anyway?"

"Over the next hill. At that stump she calls Stumpy."

"Mom, I think you should let me and Tina go to school in town."

Her mother watched her feet one slow step at a time.

"No offense," Lucy added.

"I know," Mallory said. She didn't seem angry. More like relieved. "Let me work on your dad."

Lucy's phone buzzed. A text from Noah. Here. At the cabin? Why so early?

She scrolled to the message above and saw a text

that Lucy had sent but not sent: *Hey why don't you come at like 5:30? Can't wait to see you!*

Lucy was gasping, out of breath but also out of words. Unable to speak in part because a leaden weight dropped in her gut; a churning, cold feeling. Unable in part because Mallory—Mother—was seemingly reading Lucy's mind and shouting the very words that were lodged in Lucy's throat: *Why? What? Tina?*

In a clearing stood a birch stump, waist high. Wild-flowers arranged on the ground in a semicircle in pretty patterns of blue, yellow, and gold. And in the center of the semicircle, a black rabbit with no head.

The head perched atop the stump, smiling.

The workshop door stood open so no popping of sticky wood when Beck stumbled in. His mind went jagged; he could only see in impressionistic smears and what he saw was a boy in white kissing his naked daughter. Ropes draped between them like tinsel. His first thought was *how cold she must be on the floor in this dank heartbroken place, this place where heads of boys and girls are stolen, this dusky hole in the wildness that tricks us into believing we can build a safe place for tomorrows, the only problem being that wildness isn't a location and tomorrows are yesterdays and todays are never here.*

Sweat stinging his eyes, Beck felt himself grabbing the boy. Gripping him by the fabric of his shoulders and pulling like yanking a tree root from the ground, that much force. He pulled mightily and when the root came free the tree was flung backward and crashed hard into the peg board with the whole room quaking as tools escaped their hooks and rained thunder on that boy's head.

Beck grunted, punched by a stabbing pain in his ribs; stinging deep violation.

Tina had slid a knife into him, her nude body taut and hairless as a little boy, hair spraying from her head like fireworks. She drew out the blade, excruciating, a kitchen knife. Tomatoes, onions, garlic, blood.

Don't take him from me.

She spoke these words or perhaps My Lord I will wait for thee, for thee, I want you inside me so I will never stray.

And she wielded the knife exactly like that man in the famous black-and-white movie, the man who was a woman was a man—mother and son together in one—downward stabs, leading with her hand heel as if banging on a door to be let in and Beck was the door.

Noah made the world again.

Noah the sex boat.

Noah the womb of humanity.

Painted like a slaughterhouse, she thought, although Lucy had never seen a slaughterhouse. The phrase settled into her head like a tick. Her father lay face down in a spreading pool, a dark pool like a portal widening to draw him inside. Tina sat pale and unclothed on Noah's lap, Noah propped against the wall with eyes closed and an axe in his head.

Mother rushed to Beck, a hopeful and euphonious groan ushering from her throat, but Lucy could see that her father was dead. Still as clay.

Tools from the peg board had crashed on and around Noah and Tina. The axe blade stood wedged in his skull; his tuxedo blood-draped. When Lucy dragged Tina to the center of the room, Tina kicked and tried to bite her hand. On closer look she saw that the blade wasn't buried deeply—half an inch; it dislodged from his matted scalp but blood was oozing fast. He opened his eyes to regard her with a dazed expression. Lucy tore off a length of dress and tied it around his head.

Mother and Tina formed a clumsy tangle of arms, half-tackle half-hug, as Lucy helped Noah to his feet. Tina, pinned by Mother, shivered from chill or shock or anger and from her lips came the sad tune of the whistler. Lucy bore most of Noah's weight on her shoulder, towing him to the door, to moonlight. Tina issued noises, a coiled braid of squeals and growls, an erasure of language skinned to the bones of despair.

"I've got you," Lucy was saying, her voice foreign in her ears. "We're getting out of here."

She started the engine, whirled the Cherokee in a circle toward the gap in the trees. Noah lay fading in the backseat as Lucy guided them like a dream into the fingers of the gray forest.

Headlights open the darkness. The way out, the way in. This tunnel, this vein.

She has no thought of where she is going, only of lives to save.

Nothing wasted, nothing tragic. No sadness nor tears.

Threads of dead they touch your head.

Answer without answer.

Lucille in time, in time.

Moving south, then east, train and bus, town to town following a line she couldn't see, hiding her condition for as long as she could under baggy clothes. In one village she cleaned tables, in another hotel rooms. When discovering she was with child they always cut ties, pitying without sympathy, scorn clouding their features.

The boy was born at a Quaker village. They took Lucille in and the midwife kept her tended. In the throes of delivery Lucille spit-laughed at the irony, causing the midwife to briefly think she was going septic. The baby was laid upon her breast writhing, a lumpen thing that stirred only relief that it was finally out of her. The midwife asked what he would be called. Lucy had no name because to name him would be to give him what she never had. The midwife suggested one from the Bible. "A strong name," she said. In time the boy became that word for others but never for Lucille; he was skin and blood and bone and no more.

Twice she tried abandoning the boy only to have him returned.

She had to call him something, so after her father that word was Branch, what her father had become at death, a bent crooked offshoot that scrapes and jabs and is caressed by no hand. Kindling for fires of mercy or hate. She knew her boy was blameless, and this only made the hurt more deep.

In time she became the white ghost she'd seen in

visions. When War bloomed on the skin of the world she had bodies to tend, her duty to stitch and salvage all sons, brothers, and fathers crowding the beds. When the next War bloomed, she did the same. And in all the years between and after, she tended to sick and broken and dying as if salvation was possible, this illusion her retroactive penance.

She never took a husband. More accurately she was not taken, would not let herself. The only way she would have it was her own.

ACKNOWLEDGMENTS

Deep gratitude to the early-draft readers of this book, whose sage advice was much-needed : Matt Roberson and Janice Kidd. Big thanks to Pam Van Dyk for the sharp and generous editing, and to Jaynie Royal and everyone at Regal House Publishing for giving this novella a wonderful home. I also owe a debt of gratitude to Wilderness State Park (special shoutout to Nebo Cabin) and Ludington State Park, both in Michigan, whose forested landscapes were a strong source of inspiration. Finally, thanks to Courtney for everything.